TALL TALES

& Short Stories

a collection of short fiction

by

tom catalano

Enjoy!
Tom Catalano

About the author...

Tom Catalano is the author of *Rhyme & Reason*, a best-selling collection of his original humorous and sentimental contemporary poetry; and *Tall Tales & Short Stories*, a collection of his short fiction featuring fun-filled tales of mystery and imagination. His work has appeared in dozens of poetry publications, anthologies, and newspapers. He has read his work at leading bookstores and community events throughout the midwest. He studied creative writing at Aurora University in Aurora, Illinois and has written novels, short stories, stage plays, poetry, and songs. ☐

Acknowledgements...

Thanks to **John Dall**, **Margie Fazio**, and **Keith Niemeyer** for their artistic vision; to **Fr. James Schwab** for his input; and to all the people who bought ***Rhyme & Reason*** and then came back and told me that I had touched their lives. Most of all, thanks to my family for believing in me. □

to my wife, my most loyal fan
&
*to my mother, who has stood
beside me all the way*

First Edition
Copyright ©1995 by Thomas E. Catalano

Tall Tales & Short Stories is a collection of 13 works of fiction. The characters in them have been invented by the author, and any resemblance to actual persons, living or dead, is purely coincidental. The stories are also fictitious.

All rights reserved. No part of this work covered by the copyright hereon may be reproduced in any manner whatsoever or used in any form without written permission from the publisher.

Printed in the United States of America

Published by:
Wordsmith Books, P.O. Box 7394, Villa Park, Illinois 60181

CONTENTS

Two Sleds 9

The Carrier 15

Harry's Hit 25

The Blessing 35

Widowmaker 45

Tennessee 55

Telephone Madness 65

Something's In The Basement 73

Brother Edwin 83

Clementine's Yard 95

The Last Alternative 105

The Big "L" 113

Merry New Christmas 137

Two Sleds

As I stared out the window at the new fallen snow that still needed to be shoveled, I chanced to see two young children pass by the front of my house dragging their sleds behind them. The taller of the two, a girl, was bundled up in a pink hooded jacket and pants. A scarf, wrapped around her neck, covered her nose and mouth. The boy, seemingly her younger brother, followed close behind. He wore a gray hooded jacket and a scarf which partially covered his face also. I wondered how far their mother had gotten in their dressing process before one of them decided that they had to go to the bathroom.

I smiled as I watched these two young children, who were wrapped up like a couple of pin cushions, head toward the local snow-covered park. The red molded plastic sleds that they dragged behind them looked to be more bulky than heavy. Nevertheless, just beyond my driveway, the big sister stopped. She looked back at her little brother who was dragging his sled quite contently. The sled was nearly twice as long as he was tall, but he didn't seem to mind.

Deciding that the sled must be too heavy for him, she did what any older sibling might do — offer assistance. From the window I could not hear the offer or the reasoning behind it, but she explained her position and then attempted to take the sled from him. He resisted, naturally, and started to cry. It was a pathetic sight. Her, yelling at him and trying to yank away his sled to do the sisterly thing and carry it for him. And him, crying and holding on for dear life to a sled that he might have gotten for Christmas. What had undoubtedly started out as a me-and-my-sister-are-going-sledding adventure, had developed into a test of wills and strength.

With a hearty shove, the girl sent her brother sprawling in the snow. With great resolve, she placed the form-fitting sled on top of her own and started to drag them both behind her as if nothing had happened.

The brother would have none of that. It was *his* sled and he should be able to carry it if he wanted to. He stood from the snow, red-faced and teary-eyed. With an equal amount of resolve, he began walking home in the opposite direction. His pace was quick but he never ran. He would not give Sis the satisfaction. As he passed back in front of my house I could see that he had not brushed off the snow which covered his back and legs. Evidence for Mom, no doubt.

Sis stopped and shouted after him. "Where are you going?" I imagined her saying. "Don't you want to go to the park? I'm going to go without you. You'll see, I will. Baby!"

Brother never turned, never slowed, and as far as I could tell, never answered. "Let's see what Mom has to say," I imagined him thinking. "She can't push me around. Who does she think she is? Why can't I have any fun too?"

Within moments he was out of view. She stood motionless with the two sleds as he stormed down the block.

I left the window, intending to return to my chores, but I couldn't shake the incident from my mind. It reminded me of my own comparable, although not identical, sibling rivalries of years ago. For instance, there was the time that my younger brother wanted nothing more than to "hang around" with me one summer afternoon. I loved him, of course, there was no question of that, but there was nearly five years between our ages and I had just wanted to spend time with my friend Skippy, who was closer to my own age.

"Where are you going?" he asked.

"You can't come," I remember telling him.

"Why not? Where are you going?"

I fabricated a long tale of how the Earth had been invaded by a huge Moby Dick-type monster and how Skippy and I were going to go off and save the world. Or the whale, I can't remember which.

"I want to go, too!"

"You can't. It eats little kids just like you," I told him, even though I wasn't much bigger myself then.

"I don't care," he said as he started to cry. "I want to go, too! I'm telling Mom!"

My brother went in the house to plead his case and I went off to 'save the world.' Even then, I regretted having done and said what I did. He was a sweet, if not sometimes feisty, little kid who just wanted to be 'grown up' like his older brother. But at that age there wasn't room enough for budding friendships and a tag-along brother.

It makes me sad now to think of how incidents like that one cause siblings to grow further and further apart. Then one day, after they've grown up, one or both of them looks back on their life and wonders why they were never close. I thank God this didn't happen with us. Whether it was insightful direction by our parents, or some deep down instinct on my part, we shared enough common adventures so that we grew up happy and close. Today we enjoy a friendship closer than any I have known; and I don't even know where Skippy lives anymore.

After ten minutes or so, I took another look outside

and could see the girl still standing where her brother had left her. There was no sight of him. As I watched her, wondering how long she would wait, he came into view. He was walking at the same quick pace and with the same determined resolve that he had when he headed home. What did Mom say about it? Was she even told? It didn't matter, little brother knew what he was going to do. I stood fixed at the window, anxious to find out what that was.

When he reached her, only a few words were said. Then Sister lifted the front end of the two sleds and Brother lifted the back. Together they carried their sleds down the sidewalk toward the park.

A perfect solution, I thought. No disappointments, and no less fun. How they arrived at that outcome didn't matter. What mattered was knowing that even though it wouldn't be the last time they quarreled, there were peaceful alternatives. They found theirs, and with a little luck will remember the next time. And there *will* be a next time...because big sisters watch out for their little brothers, and because every so often Moby Dick invades the Earth.

# # #

The Carrier

The year was 2038. After the Great Economic Decline ten years ago, there was a great surge of new births across the nation. Food, grown on government-controlled habitats, was rationed to try and accommodate the phenomenal increase in population. This increase posed a multitude of problems for society.

There were so many new drugs and techniques available to physicians that life expectancy was extended, but the quality of life wasn't being improved proportionately. In fact, many people felt that science was capable of actually halting death, without giving any real thought or compassion to terminally ill patients or their families.

A great debate raged in legislative chambers across the country on whether to limit the number of births per family. Just when it seemed that lawmakers would pass such legislation, a scientist in Geneva, Switzerland discovered a way to use hypnosis to induce euthanasia — mercy killing. The procedure, called 'The Carrier Method of Euthanasia (CME),' was intended to painlessly and compassionately resolve the growing problem of overcrowding caused by dying people who wouldn't die.

The procedure was a simple one. The patient, and someone who was familiar to that patient, were both put in a deep hypnotic state while lying near each other. While under hypnosis, the patient's 'carrier' was instructed to make a mental connection with the patient. The patient was instructed to accept direct commands from their carrier. At that moment, both the carrier and the patient were in a deep state of unconsciousness. Through a hypnotic 'joining,' the carrier provided the mental strength for the patient to release their grip on life and to cross over into death. After the patient slipped willingly and painlessly into death, the carrier was then brought out of the hypnotic state.

Of all the physicians in Willow County, Dr. James Emery was the one who most favored CME. Although he had at first rejected the procedure because of the possible risk involved, he later recognized it as the medical breakthrough that it was. "No risk is too great if it benefits the whole of society," his colleagues had convinced him. And CME certainly did. It was radical in concept, but it swept the nation as being the optimum entry into the hereafter. It was natural, painless, and best of all, it was swift. At last there was mercy available for terminally ill and comatose victims.

The cool autumn wind whistled through the shutters of Grandmother's house as Mother, Father, Aunt Clara, Cousin Jesse, and I waited for Dr. Emery to emerge from her room. She'd been comatose ever since suffering a stroke. At seventy-nine years old, there was little hope for her recovery. Several physicians had examined her and agreed, and yet, they each had prescribed a half dozen 'miracle pills' to keep her alive. Each night we would pray that her departure would be natural...and soon, to end the suffering she felt, or would feel should she wake. But each morning her heart still held life — weak and unchanged, but beating nevertheless.

The doctor had been examining her for close to an hour, and we were all anxious to get on with the procedure if, in fact, that was to be his recommendation.

"Why must we wait anyway?" Jesse asked. "It's been all over the news, why can't we just go ahead and do it ourselves?"

Aunt Clara glared at her thirty-six year old son. "Because it's against the law without a physician present. That's why."

She closed her eyes and rested her head against the back of the chair. She was more agitated than usual, understandably so. Grandmother's condition had left all of us ill at ease.

Jesse stood from the couch and shook his head. "I just want to get it over with," he said. "This waiting is terrible."

"The state insists that a licensed Euthanasist conduct the ceremony," Father said. "Emery is the finest available. He shouldn't be much longer."

But after another forty-five minutes the doctor still hadn't come out. I was nervous, so I lit another cigarette and threw the match into an already full ashtray.

"Y'know...," Jesse said to me, smug as usual, "smoking's illegal. You're lucky you don't get caught. The black market must make a fortune off of you!"

Finally the door to Grandmother's room opened and Emery stepped out. He held his suit coat and black med kit in one hand as he wiped his brow with the other. His sleeves had been rolled above the elbow and he took a moment to stroke his black and gray beard. We all watched intently as he removed a gold antique pocketwatch from his vest to see how long it had been.

"This watch belonged to my great-grandfather," he said. "Can't seem to part with it. I've gone through dozens of those fancy solar ones they have now. They never worked right. This one, though, just keeps on ticking along." He sighed and returned it to his pocket.

"Doctor?" Father asked, as we all stood, ready to welcome the doctor's suggestion.

He held up his hands. "Be patient," he said. "Please."

We all sat back down.

"Mrs. Shuester has been like this for how long now? Four months?"

"Yes sir," Father answered.

"With no change," Jesse added.

Emery nodded several times and stroked his beard. "You have undoubtedly summoned me personally because you have already decided to perform a mercy killing."

I swallowed hard and saw Aunt Clara bring her hand up to cover her mouth. Mother gripped Father's forearm, as she too felt the impact. It was both embarrassing and cruel to describe our intentions in that way. To hear a noted physician use outdated, not to mention biting, grammar was shocking. For the first time since we talked about the possibility of using a carrier, I felt pangs of guilt.

"I'm sure you feel it is the best decision," Emery said, seeing our reaction.

"Doctor...do you feel there is any chance she could recover?" Father asked. "Any chance at all?"

Emery shook his head. "I don't believe there is."

I rose and took the last drag off my cigarette. "But there is *some* chance?" I asked, dying the butt out in the ashtray.

Emery looked at me with his strong, fatherly dark eyes and smiled ever so slightly. "Son, I've been a physician for thirty-two years. I've been an Euthanasist for the past fifteen. In all that time I've learned that only one thing is certain — you can't be certain about the hereafter."

Aunt Clara started to rise, but chose instead to sit poised on the edge of her chair. "If there is some hope, surely we can't use a carrier." She glanced quickly around the room to each of us to see if we were in agreement.

Father knew that in spite of what anyone said or felt, it would be he and his sister Clara who would decide on the fate of their mother.

"Doctor, what is your opinion of the situation?" he asked, cautiously.

"My dear fellow," Dr. Emery said to Father, a man not much younger than himself, "the state has permitted me the authority to induce painless death through the Carrier Method. It is a method with which I am well-practiced and quite skilled. You no doubt have had Mrs. Shuester examined by your private physician, and he has answered that question with the same degree of uncertainty. Death is inevitable, as it is to us all. *That* I know for certain. Will she come out of the coma? And if she does, will she be restored to a normal state? It is unlikely, but who knows. Certainly we have medicines that will keep her alive for quite a while longer. If you would like I can prescribe some TXL-11, which will keep her heart pumping, but..."

Emery slowly removed his thin wire-rimmed glasses, and raised his eyebrows. For the first time that evening he seemed genuinely compassionate. "I will bid as you wish, but the decision, I'm afraid, sadly rests with the family. Just keep this in mind. Whatever decision you make, you will have to live with it. When someone questions your decision, as some relative probably will, you must be prepared to look them in the eye and say with conviction that you did what you did for *her* benefit."

Father sat down with his back to Emery. He looked up at his sister, but she still had her hand to her mouth unable to speak. She'd never been a tower of strength, and this crisis didn't help matters. Mother looked concerned and worried. Father knew that the decision would ultimately be his.

"Doctor..."

"I must warn you, the procedure is not entirely risk-free." Emery began to pace. "Mrs. Shuester is close to death. For all practical purposes she is not living, but on the other hand, she is not dead either. She is trapped within her coma. A prisoner of her own body."

"Yes, yes we know," Jesse interrupted, impatiently.

Aunt Clara's sharp look sat him back down.

"In a way, her body refuses to let her die mercifully. It keeps her from slipping over that very fine line that separates life from death. And because she cannot cross that line by herself, she floats just beyond it's grasp."

"At death's proverbial door," Jesse whispered.

Doctor Emery's poise and eloquence radiated the room. He never once lost his professional composure and that, above all else, impressed me. He'd obviously delivered the same speech hundreds of times before to confused families, and that was reassuring. But his cool mention of death frightened me a little. Not the fact of death, per se, but the coolness.

"A carrier of your choosing will lie beside Mrs. Shuester, and under the deepest hypnotic state ever explored by man, will use their strength and courage to mentally carry her soul over that fine line into death. That is the most simple way to explain it."

Aunt Clara gasped. The neighbor from down the road

had 'carried' his wife when she became terminally ill, so we were vaguely knowledgeable of the procedure, but suddenly it felt unnaturally godlike. Father patiently awaited the word of caution.

"The danger, Doctor?" Jesse interrupted.

Dr. Emery continued. "The carrier, being that close to the actual state of death, faces the possibility of being drawn over the line also."

Jesse's face suddenly turned pale. *He* had hoped to be the heroic carrier.

"I'll admit that the chance of this happening is a small one, maybe only one percent of the cases, but the risk is there."

"After...," Father started to ask.

Emery began to pace again. "After she has...crossed over, her heart will cease and I will bring the carrier out of the hypnotic state. There are no aftereffects, and the entire process should take less than an hour."

Father stared down toward the floor, deeply troubled. His eyes were tired, his emotions drained. He hadn't slept for two days, and it began to take its toll. It saddened me to watch him struggle over this decision.

"Dr. Emery," I asked, "when would you need to know?"

"Immediately, I'm afraid. I must fly to Vienna tomorrow for a conference, and I'm not planning on being anywhere near this region again for the next three months. If we are to perform the euthanasia, we must do so at once."

Aunt Clara began to sob. "Jimmy...we have to decide, we have to talk about this."

"There's nothing to decide," Father said, softly. "Doctor, we'll do it. And I will be the carrier."

"Jim!" Mother exclaimed.

Jesse looked relieved that no one was going to hold him to his original offer to 'carry' Grandmother.

"Father?" I began to ask, somewhat startled.

He held up one hand. "This is how it should be. I am her eldest, I want to personally release her."

Mother hugged him tightly and gently kissed his cheek. He took a moment to kiss her back.

"You understand the danger?" Emery asked.

"I do," he answered, without hesitation. He then followed the doctor into the room.

Again, we found ourselves waiting. Emery wouldn't let anyone into the room during the hypnotism, but promised to call us when Father was coming out of his trance. "There won't be much to see," Emery warned, "but it is always favorable to have family members near when one comes back."

While we were waiting, I smoked four or five cigarettes. I would have kept going, too, if I hadn't smoked the last of them.

Fifty minutes after Father went into the room, Emery called us in, after instructing us to be as quiet as possible.

Aunt Clara made an unconscious panting sound in her throat when she walked in, as if she was going to cry again, or faint. But the doctor softly reminded her that she would have to be perfectly silent or leave the room. She chose to leave. Jesse quickly volunteered to tend to her.

I have to admit, it was a rather unnerving sight. Father and Grandmother were lying side by side, each looking like they would open their eyes and sit up at any moment. Mother and I both prayed that Father soon would.

With his medscope, Emery listened to Grandmother's chest. He stood hunched over her for nearly ten minutes.

"This is most unusual...," he said, as he quickly grabbed her thin wrist to check her pulse. "No...no!" he shouted, as Mother and I looked on, helplessly.

Suddenly, Grandmother's eyelids fluttered open. Emery quickly turned to Father's side and began rescue operations, as Grandmother spoke feebly. "I...I just had the strangest dream. I was locked in a long dark corridor that had a light at the far end, and no one knew I was there. I called out, but no one heard. When I tried to walk, I couldn't move. Then, Jimmy appeared and pushed me down the hall until I was out. Isn't that the strangest thing?"

Dr. Emery knew that it wasn't. He'd seen it one percent of the time.

# # #

Harry's Hit

Harry Ackerman survived his wife Marie. In fact, at eighty years old, he survived almost everyone he knew. They'd remained childless by choice, so he felt very much alone when she passed away recently.

Throughout most of their sixty-one years of marriage, they had lived modestly in a small one bedroom apartment in an older part of town, saving their money for some undecided rainy day. Now, with Marie gone, Harry had no one to leave their 'nest egg' to. There was no one to share the remainder of his years with — or even anyone who would talk pleasantly about him after he was gone. It was not the first time he regretted not having children. It was ironic, he thought, that their decision to remain childless was to spare their offspring from an imperfect world. Now, there would be no one to entrust the world to after he was gone.

The days following Marie's death were dark and depressing. While sifting through the closets and boxing her belongings, Harry wondered how long it might be before a stranger was doing the same thing for him.

One of the items that he came across was their high school yearbook. With each page he turned, Harry noted the many faces of people he'd remained friends with over the years. Nearly all had since moved away and stopped writing, or died. Of the many faces he recognized, Joel Berns evoked the most emotion. As he stared at the childlike face of his lifelong rival, Harry recalled dozens of their high school confrontations, and the memories still made him angry.

Joel was good looking and athletic in those days, and

quite a lady's man. But he was also mean and spiteful, full of jealousy and malice. For whatever reason, he'd taken an instant dislike of Harry. On many occasions, he deliberately tried to break up Harry's dating relationships by trying to get the girl to fancy *him* instead.

When they both ran for senior class president, a position Joel readily admitted was of interest only to prevent Harry from having it, the campaign turned ugly. Joel openly spread rumors and lies about Harry's principles and sexual orientation. It was just enough of a distraction that Harry spent more time defending himself than talking about the issues. Joel handily won the election.

After graduation, they each enlisted in the army. They'd both been promoted to sergeant, but it was Joel who was decorated for an act of heroism while on a dangerous mission. During a fierce battle, an officer was badly hurt and unconscious. Under heavy enemy fire, Harry unselfishly risked his life and pulled the officer to safety. During the officer's hospital stay, however, it was Joel who stepped forward and claimed the act for himself.

Even Marie's affection was once the target of their rivalry. Harry overcame and married her, but not without a fight. He received threatening phone calls for months afterwards. Although the caller never identified himself, Harry knew who it was. At their high school reunion ten years later, Joel told Harry how things would have been different if *he'd* won Marie's heart. "For one thing," he said, "it wouldn't take *me* so long to figure out how to make babies!"

Neither Harry nor Joel ever moved from the small town they had grown up in. When they happened upon each other around town, they ignored all the normal pleasantries. It was always a cold and uncomfortable moment, but even the shortest of conversations provided Joel ample opportunity to insult Harry.

"Still living uptown, I see," Joel said once. "*I* managed to move away from there years ago!" On another occasion, he told Harry, "Be sure to tell Marie that when she comes to her senses, I'll be waiting. Then I'll show her what a real man is."

Harry could never quite figure out why Joel was like that. Sometimes there's just no explaining why some people dislike other people, he thought. All he knew was that every chance meeting with Joel resurrected those hateful memories. It was a series of ongoing skirmishes that they had kept alive over the years for some unknown reason, and Marie wanted no part of it. As far as she had been concerned, their rivalry was childish and should have been buried the night of graduation. "Why do you let him get to you?" she would ask. "He's not worth the baggage you carry."

She was right, Harry thought. She was always right about such matters. But he couldn't help feeling that Joel Berns had made a lifelong career of belittling and ridiculing him. Worse yet, he constantly felt pressured to defend his relationship with Marie to him. It was silly, to be sure, but that was the kind of person he'd become after a lifetime of badgering from Joel. Even after Marie's death, Joel didn't let up. An arrangement of flowers arrived at the funeral home with a card that read: 'The wrong one went.'

"He's not worth the baggage you carry," he imagined her saying. "He's just not worth it."

Now that Marie was gone, there was no one to tell him how foolish he was for feeling such hate and resentment. No one to hold his hand and remind him that it was *he* who was the victor in everything he did.

Harry set the yearbook aside and wept.

The next morning, Harry arose with a vigor and purpose he'd not felt in years. On a pad of paper he wrote out a list of things to do that day: 1) lawyer, 2) bank, 3) Carmen Roarke.

The meeting with his lawyer was a short one. With Marie gone, it was time to update his will. Having no living relatives, his beneficiaries were to be a dozen charities he and Marie favored.

The next stop was the bank where he withdrew $20,000 in large bills from his savings account. He put half the money in a large envelope and placed it in his briefcase. The other half was put into a newly opened safe deposit box.

The last item on his list was the most evasive and, without a doubt, the most dangerous. Carmen Roarke was a thirty-nine year old part-time construction worker and full-time criminal who grew up down the block from the Ackerman's. Harry knew Carmen and his family fairly well. Marie had even baby-sat for Carmen until he became an adolescent. It was then that Carmen's parents got divorced and he grew more incorrigible and delinquent. Relatively harmless childish pranks developed into shoplifting, grand theft, and then armed robbery. By the age of thirty, Carmen had spent more time in reformatories and prison than he had spent out. In spite of (or maybe because of) Carmen's colorful background, Harry and Marie always said hello whenever they saw him.

Harry knocked on Carmen's door, trembling a little. Carmen, a strapping man over six feet tall, opened the door and stood towering before Harry.

"Are you Carmen? Carmen Roarke? I'm Harry Ackerman from down the block. Maybe you don't remember me..."

Carmen nodded. "Sure I remember you, Mr. A! It's been a long time. What's up?"

"Carmen, my boy, may I speak with you a moment about something which is important to me?"

"Sure, Mr. A. C'mon in."

Harry stepped around the large young man and sat on the couch in the living room.

"Sorry to hear about Mrs. A," Carmen said, still standing. "She was all right."

"Yes, she was," Harry said. "She always thought...highly of you."

Carmen laughed. "Yeah, I remember she was baby-sitting me one time and I tried to cop a couple of bucks out of her purse when she wasn't looking. Well, she caught me and cuffed me upside my head. God, she had guts. Nobody did *that* to me before. Or ever again, either!"

Harry laughed nervously.

"But she never called the cops. Didn't even tell my mom. I never forgot that. Anyway, what can I do for you, Mr. A?"

"Carmen, I'm an old man, and I don't know how much time I've got left. I've lived a long and happy life, mind you. Not many regrets. But now Marie is gone and there's a void. We had no children, as you know. Never even had a dog. And now when I look forward, there's no one to serve as my beneficiary. Nothing to leave behind. That's a troubling thought for an old man, Carmen. The charities will get my money and they'll be happy to get it, I'm sure. But it'll be spent in short order and I'll soon be forgotten. I've realized that I will have come and gone in this world and left nary a mark.

"I would like to pass on knowing that I did something to better the world and I need your help, Carmen. I've decided that since I can't bring something into the world to make it a better place, I'll make it better by taking something *out*."

Harry pulled the envelope out from inside his jacket and set it on the coffee table in front of him.

"There's $10,000 in that envelope," he said. "Unmarked bills. I want someone to have that money. To use it to start a new life, perhaps. There's another $10,000 locked in a safe deposit box. That same person will receive a key for that box as reward for the completion of my final request in life."

"What's that?" Carmen asked.

Harry paused before answering. "I request the demise of my nemesis Joel Berns," he said, finally.

Carmen nodded, then shrugged his shoulders. "I don't know what that means."

"I want you to put the hit on Joel Berns," Harry answered.

Carmen's eyes widened. "Are you serious?! You want to whack old man Berns?! But why me? I don't have anything against the old guy."

"I don't care who does it. I just didn't know who else to ask. You don't just take an ad out in the paper about this type of thing. I don't care how, that would be up to you...or whomever does it. If you're interested, that's fine, otherwise maybe you can make a recommendation."

Carmen sat down across from Harry and thought for a moment. "Ten now, ten after...hmm. But why do this? I mean, why don't you just ignore the old guy. Why should you care if he lives or dies?"

"It's the ultimate revenge. For all the years of aggravation. And for all the times that Marie felt uncomfortable because of his sick humor. Like I said, I want to do something that will better the world. And the moment he's gone the better it will be."

"And what if...you know, you go before he does?" Carmen asked.

"Then you keep the $10,000. No one will ever be the wiser."

Carmen shook his head. "I don't like this whole thing. No sir, I don't like it at all. But, if you're dead-set on having it done, let *me* do it for you. I sort of owed Mrs. A for not turning me in. She was always real nice to me."

Harry smiled and they shook hands.

As he lay in bed that night, Harry thought about what he had arranged. How could he be certain that Carmen would hold to his promise? What would prevent him from keeping the money and not carrying out the deed? Nothing, except that as far as criminals were concerned, Harry thought Carmen to be a fairly honest one.

He smiled and then laughed as he thought of how surprised Joel would be with Carmen standing before him ready to end his life. "This is from Harry Ackerman, you dirty rat," Harry imagined him saying. "You've tried to best him all his life. This time you lose!"

As he was about to fall asleep, Harry thought that he heard a noise in the living room. Footsteps? The sound of his bedroom door slowly swinging open made him sit upright.

A tall dark figure stood in the shadows at the foot of the bed. Harry reached over and turned on the lamp.

"Carmen! You about scared the life out of me, boy."

"Sorry to wake you, Mr. A. But I had to come right over."

"What's the meaning of this, Carmen? I thought you understood the arrangements. You're not changing your mind, are you son?"

"No sir," Carmen replied. "I always keep my word. That's one thing anybody can say about me — I keep my word."

"Good. I'm counting on you."

It was then that Harry noticed a glint from the .38 revolver Carmen held at his side.

"What is this? Isn't the money enough? I am not a wealthy man."

"The money is quite generous, sir. In fact, because you're a friend, I probably would have done it for free."

"If it's the idea of committing a crime, I didn't mean any offense..."

"No, it's nothing like that," Carmen said softly.

"Then I don't understand. Why the gun?"

Carmen was motionless. "It's about Berns."

"Is he...?"

Carmen nodded. "Dead."

Harry went completely numb. His mind raced through dozens of emotions. He wasn't sure if he was happy or sorry. Had he done the right thing? What a question, he thought! How could the taking of someone's life be the 'right thing'?! It was all so confusing. Nevertheless, there was no turning back the events of the evening. What happened, unfortunately, happened. He began to tremble. "So soon?" he forced himself to say. "I had no idea it would be so soon."

"It was a heart attack. I had nothing to do with it."

"Oh," Harry said, feeling a tremendous sense of relief.

"I went to his house to do the deed. He was sleeping. As I got closer to his bed, the floorboards creaked and he sat up, just like you did. The shock of someone standing above him in the dark in the middle of the night was just too much for him, I guess. He grabbed his chest and that was that."

Harry looked down at the pistol that still hung at Carmen's side — obviously the weapon he'd chosen to 'do the deed.' It was eerie knowing that Carmen really would have pulled it off. But in a way, he was glad it never came to that. As much as he hated Joel Berns, he knew Marie would not have approved.

"In that case, you go ahead and keep the money anyway," Harry told him.

"It's not that simple," Carmen said. "Old man Berns came to see me a couple of months before *you* did and arranged his own final request. Upon his death I was to pay *you* a visit. And like I said, I always keep my word. So here I am. He had a message for you, though. He said to say, 'I win again, old friend.'"

Carmen slowly lifted his arm and pointed the revolver.

Harry closed his eyes and smiled. "It's nice to be remembered," he thought.

# # #

The Blessing

Connie was still sleeping when he woke. He didn't sleep well, and he knew why. For the first time in many years, he had to face the day without a job.

As he stretched and rubbed the life back into his eyes, he recalled the conversation he had with his boss, Mr. Aaron. His heart sank as he thought about yesterday's conversation. It was a short, but tense, few moments with the Senior Vice President.

"I'm sorry, Dave," he said, politely, "but we're going to have to let you go."

"It must be some sort of a joke," Dave remembered thinking. "They wouldn't let *me* go. I'm too valuable, too dedicated."

"The word came down that all departments have to cut back. The economy, you know. You're a fine person and a hard worker, we all know that, but there are others who have more seniority. I'm sorry."

Sorry! It was such a hard, cursory word, without thought or concern for a person's pride, he thought. It rang through his head over and over as a constant reminder that he'd failed in some way.

He felt he'd been lucky throughout his life up to that point. He'd had steady jobs, made a fairly good salary, and had made job changes whenever *he* wanted. The tide, however, seemed to be changing. Suddenly, he was faced with a job change that, for the first time in his life, wasn't his doing. He couldn't help but be concerned; he was 36 years old with a wife and two small children to support. It was July, and the summer months were traditionally the worst times of the year to look for work. It depressed him to think about it, so he did not dwell on it.

"Dave...?"

"Nothing, dear. Go back to sleep."

She didn't know yet. There was no reason she should, he thought. He would find another job somewhere in a day or two and then he would tell her. He would just say that he had wanted a change.

If it was difficult to admit the truth to his wife, it was even harder to admit it to himself. After six years of service with his company, he had begun to feel that his job was secure. It was crushing to discover that it was not.

He followed his regular morning procedures routinely. He showered, shaved, got dressed, and sat down with a cup of coffee as he collected his thoughts. The only difference was that *this* morning he did it all an hour earlier than usual. He had a lot to do and wanted to get started before the alarm went off and Connie got up. He certainly could have lied to her, but it wasn't his nature to do so. Besides, she had a keen sixth sense that told her when things were not as they should be. She had already suspected that something was wrong when he came home yesterday evening twenty minutes earlier than usual.

"I wasn't feeling well, so I left early," he had told her. It was only a little white lie, because he really *wasn't* feeling well after he was fired. In fact, it felt a lot like having been kicked in the stomach. She believed it and it gave him an excuse to be on edge for the remainder of the evening.

He closed the front door of their house quietly behind him. Once he reached the car in the driveway, he knew he would be safe — no questions and no lies. In ten or fifteen minutes the alarm would go off and Connie would get up to start her day. She would assume that he went into the office a little early as he had so many times before.

The first order of the day was to file for benefits at the Bureau of Unemployment. There was always that possibility that he would not find employment as quickly as he hoped. If he didn't, he had to be certain that his family would have *some* income — even if it was only a small percentage of what he had been earning.

The unemployment office wouldn't be open for another hour, so Dave stopped at the local diner. He wasn't hungry, but he knew that he had better eat while he had the time. If the lines at the unemployment office were as long as he had heard, he wouldn't have another chance to eat until mid-afternoon, which would be impossible. That would mean that he wouldn't have much of an appetite at dinner, and that would be a dead giveaway to Connie that something was wrong. He thought of everything.

Before his eggs and bacon arrived, he jotted a few notes on the small note pad he carried in his briefcase. He wrote: 1) Register for unemployment compensation, 2) Call Greene Executive Placement Service for job leads, 3) Revise resume. He had just begun to write down his experience as a Quality Control Engineer, when he was interrupted.

"Hey Dave, how do?!"

He didn't even need to turn around. He recognized Stan's greeting immediately. He should, he had heard it five mornings a week for the past six years.

"Morning Stan," he answered.

"Mind if I join you?" his former co-worker asked. He didn't wait for an answer, he sat down across from Dave.

"Not at all."

Dave would have much preferred to be left alone, especially this morning. He was feeling very self-conscious about being out of work and didn't want company. But Stan was the pushy type. It had always irritated Dave. This morning it was only slightly different — it was worse.

"Sorry to hear that they let you go, old boy, you'll be missed."

"Thanks," he said, putting away the notebook.

"Now who am I going to go to lunch with? Or bullshit with? Yeah, I'm going to miss you all right." He smiled and ordered coffee when the waitress brought Dave's breakfast. "Everything works out for the best, and don't you forget that."

Dave didn't answer. He would rather have talked about the weather, or sports, or even office gossip.

"I've known a half dozen people who have told me that their getting fired was a blessing in disguise. A blessing! Can you believe that? They were forced to reevaluate what they truly wanted out of life and they had to set their sights accordingly. I'm sure you'll find it's the same way with you."

Dave assured him that it probably would, hoping to drop the subject.

"So what are your plans?" Stan asked. "Surely you have some." He began to sugar the coffee the waitress brought.

Dave felt like answering that it was none of his damn business, but he didn't. He was much too controlled for that. Too executive. He took his time and ate his breakfast.

"I have some leads," he answered finally. "Aaron's going to give me a letter of recommendation, and I've already put together a pretty impressive resume."

That was stretching the truth a bit, but he *was*

expecting a letter from Mr. Aaron.

"Very good. What else?"

Dave looked up from his coffee. He wiped his mouth with the napkin. "Don't you have to be somewhere, Stan? Like the office? It's nearly eight."

Stan looked at his wristwatch. "I've got time, Aaron doesn't make the rounds until eight-thirty. Nine, sometimes. You don't have to feel uncomfortable around me, Dave, we're friends, remember?"

Their 'friendship' had not transcended the confines of the office. They had lunch together every few days, but they never built a social relationship that went beyond five o'clock. This was a time of personal reconstruction for Dave and he *did* feel uncomfortable.

"I'm in contact with a few executive placement firms," Dave told him, reluctantly. "I'm not that worried, really."

"Good for you. You shouldn't be. You're a bright guy. There's got to be a lot of firms out there aching for your talent. You keep looking. You'll catch up with them sooner or later."

Dave resented being patronized. He motioned to the waitress that he was ready for the check and she began scribbling on her pad.

"So...where you off to from here?" Stan asked.

Dave paused before answering and laid four dollars on the table. If he stalled long enough he wouldn't have to embarrass himself by admitting that he was on his way to file for unemployment compensation. It was not something he was proud of. He never had to file before and the mere fact that he was filing *now* lowered his self-esteem. He was not an unmotivated laggard sucking the system dry, as was some people's stereotypical applicant. Rather, he was filing merely as a preventive measure.

"I have to head over to the placement service. Can't let this vacation last *too* long!" He forced himself to laugh and then he swallowed the remainder of his coffee.

"Well, good luck old buddy. Keep in touch."

Dave smiled and said that he would. He shook Stan's hand and left. It was a relief to be outside, he thought. Stan was a nice enough fellow with good intentions, but he was also arrogant and insensitive when he wanted to be. Dave sensed that Stan was glowing in the fact that he was now one of the top dogs of management. He was a survivor and was no longer shadowed by any other co-workers. Stan's time to shine was now. The thought made him a little envious.

The unemployment office was every bit as crowded as Dave had expected. Two lines had formed with about thirty people each at opposite ends of the large screening room. Green metal folding chairs, pushed closely together, lined the walls. The seating arrangement was less than adequate for all those who came to file for benefits.

Dave stood in the line marked 'Information' for fifteen minutes before receiving the necessary forms he had to fill out and present to the administration assistant when his number was called. Ordinarily, he hated waiting in lines. They were so time-consuming. Today, he didn't mind as much for he had the time to spare.

He had the forms completed within ten minutes. Now there was nothing to do until they called his number.

"One hundred thirty-three," a woman called, standing near the information desk.

Dave pulled the small ticket stub from his pocket and checked his number: one hundred eighty-four. He was glad he had eaten breakfast.

He surveyed the room and studied the various mix of people who were there applying for benefits. There seemed to be representatives from every walk of life. Surprisingly, most of the people who were waiting seemed to be a cross section of middle class America. Many of the men and women wore business suits and carried briefcases, just like Dave. "No one is immune," he thought. Every one had their lives put on hold, probably just as suddenly as *he* had. You could feel the chill in the air, and the fear. No one talked about it, but everyone knew what everyone else was feeling. In a way, it was a social club in which no one wanted to belong, and from which everyone couldn't wait to get out.

He was fascinated with trying to decipher the story of every new person who walked in. A young man wearing shorts, a tee-shirt, and athletic shoes had been out of work for some time, he concluded. A woman, middle-aged, came in next, handsomely dressed. Just fired, he figured. A nicely dressed man, around Dave's age, stood in line for the necessary forms. At a distance, Dave thought he recognized the man. He watched closely.

The man seemed awkward and nervous. He fidgeted while in the line, obviously very concerned about his future. There was little doubt that it was his first time at the unemployment office.

The man received his forms and sat down to fill them out. He was so engrossed that he didn't notice when Dave came over and sat next to him.

"Hey Stan, how do?"

Stan looked over. His eyes widened and his face flushed.

"They got you too, huh?" Dave asked.

Stan nodded. "First thing this morning. Aaron called

me in and fired me right then and there. Me, can you believe it? No warning, no 'clean up your act' speech... nothing. Just some mumbo-jumbo about my lack of productivity and blah, blah, blah. You're fired, get out. Now I'm down here begging for money just like these losers."

Stan had always been a poor judge of character, Dave thought, which is probably why they never became better friends.

"I'm dazed. I still can't get over it. I was on easy street — one of the survivors. I'd given absolutely no thought to what I'd do if *I* was on Aaron's chopping block. When *you* went, I thought I was safe. They thinned the ranks, loosened the screws. I don't know what I'm going to do now."

He looked away, ashamed, refusing to look at Dave or the forms that still needed to be completed. Both reminded him too much of the situation.

"Here's your chance to reevaluate what you truly want out of life, just like you told *me*," Dave told him. "You often complained of the way Aaron handled company affairs, here's your chance to start fresh somewhere else. Everything works out for the best. You'll see."

Stan smiled. "A blessing in disguise?"

"Sure," Dave answered. "You just have to pick yourself up, brush yourself off, and go on. What happened today was not an evaluation of your character, it was just a...setback. You've got to be strong and go on. Not only for your family but for yourself."

Stan nodded.

"Have you told Beth yet?"

Stan shook his head. "Frankly, things haven't been great on the homefront. I don't want any more friction than we already have." He pulled a cigarette from his pack, noticed a 'No Smoking' sign and put it back. "Beth has a tendency to fly off the handle over little things. And this is definitely not a little thing. She'll think I did something to deserve getting canned. Or she'll think I just out-and-out quit. Maybe with a little luck I can find another job and she'll never be the wiser." He smiled. "Yeah...that might just work! Sneaky, huh?"

"Sneaky," Dave agreed.

"How'd Connie take it?"

Dave didn't hesitate a minute to answer. "Fine, considering the suddenness and all. She was concerned, of course, but fully supportive." He knew she would be. She was nothing like Beth. She wouldn't accuse him or be suspicious. In fact, she would be strong and encouraging, just like she always was during trying times. It surprised him that it took Stan's misfortune to make him realize that about his wife.

"What do you say we go and tie one on after we take care of our business here?" Stan suggested. "I'd say we deserve it!"

Dave didn't even need to think about the offer. He pictured Connie at home with their kids, sensing that something was wrong, and worrying about him. He declined the invitation.

"Maybe some other time, Stan. Tonight I'm getting a baby-sitter and taking my wife out for a nice dinner. But let's all get together for a drink sometime."

"Sure, I'd like that," Stan said.

"I'll mention it to Connie." Among other things, Dave thought.

# # #

Widowmaker

There were other routes, of course. She'd taken Andrews Road, for instance, on many occasions, but it was much slower; only thirty-five miles per hour through town and stop-and-go most of the way. Tonight, Marla Johnson was anxious to get home. It was late and she was exhausted. The business conference ended much later than expected, and she was looking forward to just feeding her cat, taking a nice long soak in the tub, and falling into bed. She chose the faster, express route — the turnpike. The one they called 'Widowmaker.'

Widowmaker was a paved, two-lane highway, and was sure to save her a good fifteen to twenty minutes getting home. It was also more dangerous. Forty-five miles per hour was the maximum speed limit with sharp, winding turns all along the way. Many of the turns were hairpin, requiring a minimum of extreme caution. On more than one occasion the turnpike earned its nickname.

It was a routine ride, for that time of the evening. Visibility was clear and the traffic was light. She had the windows open slightly so that the crisp November air would help prevent drowsiness. Now, especially, she wanted her wits about her. The Widowmaker Turnpike was no place to be careless.

She'd been driving for about twenty-five minutes, and was only a few miles from her exit, when an 18-wheel tanker truck that was headed in the opposite direction rounded the bend. It was a wide turn. Far too wide for a road that narrow. Far too fast for a vehicle that large. Its headlights panned quickly across the pavement as it made the turn. As it crossed over the solid yellow line, both headlights flashed in Marla's face. She was momentarily blinded.

She yanked on the steering wheel. Her small car veered right, narrowly avoiding the truck. However, in doing so, she headed straight for the edge of the road...and whatever was down below.

Marla pressed hard on the brake pedal, but it didn't help. She felt the gravel of the shoulder under her wheels, and then the slide began. As she tried to steer the car back onto the pavement, the backend fishtailed forward, removing what little control she had left over the car. At that moment it was clear...she was going over. She knew it was at least seventy-five feet to the bottom of the ravine.

With a little luck, she prayed, perhaps the car would be stopped by one of the nearby trees jutting from the sloped embankment. The car would surely suffer some body damage, she thought, but at least she would be alive.

Marla frantically pumped the brakes, hoping that at any minute the sliding car would come to a stop and her biggest concern would be finding a tow truck at that time of the evening. But the car wouldn't stop. Bushes and branches were pushed aside or trampled. The headlights bounced up and down, illuminating only small patches of the dense ravine that drew her in.

The pounding and scraping shrieked through the car as she prayed for help. Suddenly, the car slid into something solid. A stump or a large rock, she figured. It hit broadside with a loud thump, sending her sprawling across the front seat. She screamed. Momentum propelled the car up and over the object, causing it to roll. She grabbed for something to hold on to but nothing was in reach. The car rolled over and over until it came to an abrupt stop.

Marla realized she must have blacked out, because she found herself on the floor when she came to. She had no idea how long she'd been there, or how much longer she would have to wait before help arrived. It was a lonely stretch of road, it could be hours before someone passed. And even if they did, chances were good that they wouldn't notice a car at the bottom of the ravine. Not at night. Especially not on a curve. It occurred to her that if she didn't try to help herself, she may very well not receive any help at all.

She climbed back onto the seat without much difficulty. Small cubes of broken glass covered the seat and floor. She brushed some of it away and slid behind the steering wheel.

"Damn!" she said aloud. "Wait until my insurance company sees this! They'll drop me for sure. Hmm...that's strange. After all that, and I haven't even broken anything. No body parts, at least. And without my seatbelt, no less! The car looks like hell, but at least I'm not in any pain. I sure lucked out this time."

"I wouldn't count on that just yet," a male voice said from outside the car. "Looks can be deceiving."

Marla turned quickly. A man in his late twenties, dressed in blue jeans and a torn tee-shirt, stood next to the passenger side of the car. She gasped.

"You startled me!"

"I'm sorry, really, I didn't mean to," he said gently. "How do you feel? Any pain?"

"No," she answered. "Are you from the highway patrol?"

The stranger smiled. "No, I'm not," he said. "But I

am here to help you."

"Do you have a car phone?"

He shook his head.

"A rope to pull the car out? A chain?"

"Sorry," he said.

"You can at least give me a ride to the next exit, can't you?"

He shrugged his shoulders.

"Well, thanks anyway, mister," she snapped. "You're a big help. But all I need right now is a tow truck and a good stiff drink."

He shook his head again. "I'm sorry to say that neither one of those is possible. You've been injured, Miss Johnson. Quite seriously, I'm afraid."

Marla smiled. "Yes, I thought I would be too. But as you can see, I'm fine. A little shook up, of course, but who wouldn't be? At least I'm all in one piece. Say...how did you know my name?"

"I checked your driver's license while you were unconscious, actually. I hope you don't mind."

"'Mind'? No, of course not. Why should I mind if someone pokes through my belongings?" she asked, sarcastically. "Find anything worth keeping?!"

"I'm not a thief, oh no. I had to know what to call you, in case you...came to."

If this guy wasn't a thief, she thought, then maybe he was a rapist. Suddenly, she was glad she woke up when she did.

"I'd better see if I can...," she began, trying the ignition.

"It won't work," he said. "And not really a good idea, anyway. Accidents often cause gasoline spills, you know, and you wouldn't want an explosion or anything."

Marla pulled her hand quickly away from the key.

"The horn won't work either," he added, just as she thought to try.

She tried anyway, but it didn't work — just as he predicted.

A wave of fear swept over her. There was something very odd about this stranger who appeared from nowhere. He seemed to know what she was going to do even before *she* did. And if he wasn't a medic or with the state police, how was he intending on helping her? The car was too far down the embankment for one man to push it out alone. If he was indeed a rapist, he had perfect timing, she thought. It wasn't bad enough just to have a car stuck at the bottom of a ravine, now she had some spooky guy hanging around.

"So, have you decided?" he asked.

"'Decided?' The only decision I have to make right now is how to get my car the hell out of here! And I don't think I've got that many choices, actually."

The young man stared at her. "Then...you don't know."

"Know what? Mister, I've had about enough of this. I've had a bad day. My boss is driving me crazy, I'm tired, I'm hungry, I've wrecked my car, and now I'm stuck at the bottom of a ravine in the middle of the night. You're talking in riddles and I'm in no mood for it."

He nodded. "You're right. If you haven't realized it yet, perhaps I should just tell you. I'm just surprised that it hasn't occurred to you."

"What?" Marla asked, again suspicious of his intentions. Then she noticed. Other than their own voices, she heard no sounds. The trees and leaves were still, the crickets were mute, the birds were silent, no traffic passed over the road — nothing made a sound anywhere.

"My, it's awfully quiet," Marla said. "This is almost like a dream. A *bad* dream! Maybe my alarm will go off in a minute and I'll have dreamed this whole thing, huh? No, I couldn't be so lucky. Maybe I'm just dead."

She started to laugh, but the man's blank expression never changed. She began to tremble. "That's ridiculous. I can't be dead. There has to be a logical explanation."

"You're right, there is," he said. "You're not dead, but I'll tell you this much, you're as close to death as anyone is ever likely to get."

"What does *that* mean? I feel just fine."

"You are at an interim, so to speak," he said. "That split moment just before you pass from this world to the next."

Marla stared at him. "Are you actually trying to tell me that..."

"You're dying."

"That's what I thought you were leading up to. Look mister, I don't know who you are, or why you're here, but if you don't mind excusing me, I have to figure out what to do about getting my car out of here."

"Miss Johnson, I don't blame you for not believing. But you must. Look around. The world has been put on hold. *Your* world, that is. Time, as you know it, has stopped. That's what happens when you are...as you are. And until you decide, that's exactly the way it's going to stay — indefinitely."

"There you go talking in riddles again. Decide *what*?"

The stranger hesitated. "Why...you need to decide whether or not to pass."

"To...'pass'?"

"To pass into the next world, Miss Johnson. To die."

"Die?! I have no intention of dying, thank you very much. Not now, at least. Not here. And I don't appreciate your sense of humor."

"No humor intended, Miss Johnson," he said. "I'm dead serious. But I wouldn't be so quick in choosing life."

Marla's nervousness grew as she once again began to fear the intruder. "I also don't appreciate being threatened."

"No, it's nothing like that," he said. "Not at all. That's what I came over to tell you. You have to understand. Whether you want to believe it or not, you *are* dying. When a person is this close to...passing, as you are, time stands still for a moment and they are given a choice. Peaceful and painless death, or survival. It's entirely their own choice."

Marla thought for a second. "If this is true...," she began, "and I'm not saying I believe it for a minute, but if what you say is true, that I really am...as you say I am, then why in the world would I choose anything but life?"

"Why? Because the life you will have chosen will be filled with pain and discomfort beyond your wildest dreams. Unless, of course, you slip into a coma. In which case, you may as well *be* dead. You see, to choose death now, while you are able, you may save yourself much suffering."

He may be right, she thought. Maybe she *was* dying. Maybe she *was* stuck in some sort of a time...freeze. That would certainly explain some very peculiar things: the absolute silence in the air, the sudden appearance of a passerby, not to mention that she didn't even suffer a bump from an accident that in all likelihood should have killed her. As much as she didn't want to believe, something told her that it might be true. Just as he said.

She began to feel that if she closed her eyes and relaxed she would indeed slip off into death. But on the other hand, if she really tried...

"I choose...to live," she said suddenly. "I want to live!"

The man nodded. "I respect your decision. I do. I only pray for *your* sake that you don't live to regret it — you won't be given a second chance to decide."

Marla's distrust of the stranger turned to dislike as she vowed a full recovery, if for no other reason than to spite him. Whoever he was.

She closed her eyes. Was it really happening, she wondered? The stranger, their conversation, the deadening silence? When she opened her eyes would it prove to have been just an illusion? Yes, it would have to be. She imagined the doctors she would soon be seeing commenting on how lucky she was to have escaped injury. That's what it was — luck. Nothing else. 'Interim,' indeed!

"Open your eyes, Miss Johnson. It's time."

No, Marla thought, it couldn't be. The voice she heard was that of the stranger. A chill ran through her.

"Miss Johnson. It was your choice. You must open your eyes in order for your decision to be binding."

Marla forced her eyelids open. Pain suddenly shot through her head before they fully opened. She tried to reach up to her face with both hands, but one arm lay motionless next to her body. Broken glass covered the floor where she found herself — still. Her arms and legs were severely bruised and possibly broken. The pain in her chest and abdomen was incredible. He'd been right.

All along the stranger had been right.

"I'm sorry, Miss Johnson. Truly I am."

Tears filled her pained eyes and streamed down her cheeks, but she didn't feel them.

"I wish you strength, Miss Johnson. You're going to need it. And I envy your courage. I'll say good-bye now. You won't be seeing me again. Don't worry, someone will be by shortly to tend to you, I'm sure."

Marla listened as the wind rustled the tree branches above the car and crickets chirped in the distance. It *was* reality. She was back.

"I'll make it, damn it!" she screamed. "I'll make it!"

"Yes...I do believe you will," the stranger said, barely loud enough for her to hear.

She did, however, clearly hear his footsteps moving away from the car.

"Wait!" she called from the floor.

He stopped.

"Before you go...please, who *are* you?"

He was silent for a moment and then answered. "Me? I was in an accident very much like yours. Not too far from here, as a matter of fact. Only *I* couldn't make up my mind."

# # #

Tennessee

No one knew what his real name was. He just showed up at the bar one day and everyone started calling him 'Tennessee.' No one could remember exactly why.

"Don't bug me," he would say, time and time again, only half conscious.

He was usually drunk when he'd say it. It was his way of avoiding conversation with everyone. It didn't matter, no one wanted to talk with him anyway. He was usually just ignored, and was only occasionally drawn into their arguments. Not that they cared much for his opinion; they thought it was fun to tease him and listen to him babble on almost incoherently. But arguing wasn't Tennessee's nature. Then again, it wasn't his nature to do much of anything other than to drink to excess.

Nine years ago, almost to the day, Tennessee's life changed dramatically. After working for the same company for more than thirty years, he suddenly found himself out of work after management had 'restructured' the organization. He was forced to look for a new job at fifty-seven years of age.

His wife of nineteen years tried to be supportive, for she could see the situation was taking a toll on her husband. On her, too. Within a year she began taking tranquilizers to calm herself and cope with a dwindling household account and a degenerating husband. One day, after 'calming' herself, she failed to stop at a red light, driving through an intersection unaware of the oncoming traffic. She was killed instantly.

Tennessee slipped into a state of depression that he never emerged from. He wasn't able to maintain the mortgage payments on their house and the bank foreclosed. At that point, he'd lost more than his job, his wife, and a house; he'd lost his self-respect. He began to drink continuously, almost making Artie's Wet Whistle, the neighborhood tavern, his permanent residence.

Artie, the owner and bartender, didn't mind him hanging around. Tennessee pretty much kept to himself and never caused any trouble. Some of the other regulars liked to have a laugh at Tennessee's expense, but they were never physically abusive.

Tennessee didn't particularly like to drink, but it helped him forget. More importantly, it helped numb the constant loneliness. Although he had a little savings tucked away, he was pretty much living off the insurance money from his wife's accident. He rarely went to Artie's with more than a few dollars. But he was a 'regular' and all the other 'regulars' were more than happy to buy him drinks.

Anyone who visited Artie's with any frequency, knew that Tennessee was a confused old man down on his luck. When he spoke, it was often in sporadic half sentences that were either unintelligible or gross exaggerations. But if anyone could take a joke, "good ol' Tennessee" sure could.

The cost of the 'complimentary' drinks was paid off many times over by having to sit through hours of their endless ridiculing. Tennessee would always answer their insensitive comments with his quick and simple, "Don't bug me." It always made them laugh. Tennessee was fun to have around.

Tennessee lived in a shabby one room apartment on the lower east side. Artie felt sorry for the old man and would let him sleep off his drunkenness in the back room on an old couch when he couldn't get home on his own.

On this particular afternoon, Artie set up another round of drinks compliments of Phil Dugan seated at the end of the bar. Tennessee slowly lifted his head and looked in Phil's direction. He had to squint, his eyes weren't like they used to be. The liquor made everything a little hazy. He wasn't sure who had bought the drink, he never was. He raised his glass of whiskey in a toast of thanks to whomever was looking. He set the glass down, and dropped his head again.

Phil winked at Artie as two other regulars, Gus and Harvey, turned toward Tennessee, awaiting the excitement that was about to follow, barely containing their laughter.

"Hey, Tennessee!" Phil called out, above the music of the jukebox.

"Don't bug me," he answered, not realizing that it was payoff time.

Gus slapped Harvey on the arm as Phil got up to give Tennessee a better look at the men's magazine he had with him. He opened it to the first pictorial and slid it across the bar leaving it just under Tennessee's bowed head. Tennessee's eyes widened as they focused on the nude photographs only inches from his face.

"How about *that*, Tennessee?" Phil asked.

Tennessee lifted his head to tell Phil that he'd rather just be left alone, but no words came out. Page upon page was turned for him, monopolizing everyone's attention. Gus and Harvey looked on from the end of the bar and began to laugh. With each new page and each new expression on Tennessee's face, the laughter got stronger.

Phil kept turning the pages without any word of encouragement or objection from Tennessee.

"Wait!" Tennessee said finally. He held Phil's wrist to

keep him from turning any more pages.

"What do you know! Tennessee found one he likes!"

Gus and Harvey grabbed their bottles of beer and hurried across the room to see which photograph had caught Tennessee's attention.

"Remind you of the old days?" Phil asked. "I'm surprised you even *remember* what a naked woman looks like!"

"I remember," Tennessee mumbled.

"You have good taste, Tennessee!" Gus said. "I always knew you was a man who could spot a pretty woman when you saw one!"

They all laughed. Everyone except Tennessee.

"I don't know about this one," Harvey began, "her boobs is too small. Keep going to the centerfold, Tennessee, and let's have a better look at her."

They all crowded around Tennessee as he slowly turned one page, and then another. The room was silent as they all looked on. Even Artie watched from behind the bar.

"Man, oh man, Tennessee, you sure can pick 'em!" Gus exclaimed. "Kind of looks like my wife."

"That don't look like your wife," Harvey argued, pointing to the centerfold that Tennessee held tightly. "And if you think it do, than you're drunker'n I gave you credit for!"

Phil laughed and ordered another round. As far as he was concerned the game was over. He was bored and his attention was moving on to something else. But when he attempted to take back the magazine, Tennessee refused to give it up.

"No!" he shouted. Everyone was stunned. "No...let me look. Please."

"Well, well, *well*! I think our very own Tennessee has fallen in love!" Harvey said.

They all started laughing again.

"Please...let me look."

"Aw, leave him alone, guys," Artie said.

"Just having a little fun," Gus told him.

"The old guy don't have much, you know that," Artie argued. "Let him have a look."

Phil began to feel sorry that he had started teasing Tennessee with the magazine. He didn't even have a good reason for doing it in the first place. He didn't dislike the old man, it was just something to break the monotony of sitting in a tavern all night. Poor Tennessee was an easy target. He knew that if he took the magazine away now there would be hurt feelings. He'd gone too far this time.

"Sure, you can look at her," Phil told him. "I know she's your favorite."

"Hey! What about *us*?!" Gus exclaimed. "We was waiting too, y'know!"

"Don't bug him," Phil said. "He needs a couple of minutes with the young lady. It's no big deal."

Tennessee stood and, with the magazine still open to the centerfold, shuffled over to one of the small tables against the wall where the lighting was better.

"Now you be careful with them pages, y'hear Tennessee?" Gus shouted. "You can look at that pretty all you want, but don't you mess up them pages!"

Gus and Harvey laughed. Phil and Artie didn't.

Tennessee wasn't listening. He'd tuned them out after they first turned to that particular pictorial.

She was beautiful; as perfect as any woman could be. Sitting naked, cross-legged on a plush white shag rug, her golden blond hair was wet and combed behind her ears. She was very attractive, but her rich blue eyes were her most captivating feature, beaming with life the longer he stared at them.

He repositioned the magazine to get an even better look at her face. It was as if he knew her. Her facial features looked strikingly familiar to those of his late wife. Oh, it wasn't her, of course, the age was wrong. The girl, Maria DuSade, looked to be about twenty-one, just the age his daughter would be. That is, if he *had* a daughter. They had talked about having children many years ago, but it never happened.

The longer he stared at her eyes, the more convinced he became that this girl was a young version of his beloved wife. A daughter, long ago given up for adoption, perhaps? Thinking back, he remembered that his wife had had an abortion many years ago during a very difficult time in their lives. Could she have delivered the baby instead and given it up for adoption without his knowledge? Was it possible? No...there *was* an abortion. He couldn't remember anymore. The past had become an alcoholic blur. He missed his old life so much that sometimes the alcohol played games with his memory.

Looking at the photo, he imagined that perhaps he *wasn't* alone in the world. That maybe, somewhere, there really could be someone who cared whether he lived or died. At that moment he wanted kinship more than anything else in the world.

It made him angry that these guys had been gawking at her. He resented them for it. He resented anyone who would purchase a magazine that had desecrated his precious little girl. What terrible things could have happened to her to take up a life as a nude model?

He wanted to tear up the magazine, to destroy all evidence of her actions, but knew he could not. It wasn't an exclusive copy, nor was it his to destroy. He knew these animals would just buy another one.

"Hey, Tennessee!" Gus called. "You about done?"

"Yeah, give *us* a chance with her!" Harvey shouted.

They laughed. That same childish laughter Tennessee heard time after time, day after day. But this time he had something they *didn't* have. He felt like a protective father, a man with substance in his life again, and he had no intention of giving that — or her — up.

Phil got up and walked over to Tennessee's table and gently placed his hand on the old man's shoulder.

"What do you say, old timer? About done with the young lady?"

There was no answer.

"Tennessee?"

Tennessee closed the magazine and put both of his large hands on top of the cover. He stared straight ahead as if no one else was around or speaking to him. But he heard what Phil was asking. Every word.

"Me and the boys would like to get some of that enjoyment too, Tennessee. If you'd like to share her, that is. You about done?"

"You can't have her back," Tennessee said, firmly.

"What do you mean we can't have her back!" Harvey exclaimed from across the room.

Phil held up his hand to quiet his friends.

"Ah...I know what you want. Artie, give ol' Tennessee another drink. On me!"

"No!" Tennessee shouted, loud enough for everyone in the bar to hear. He shook his head and continued softly.

"Thank you...but no."

"Then what *do* you want, Tennessee?"

For the first time, Tennessee looked up at Phil. "I just want you to leave my daughter alone."

Phil and Artie couldn't believe what they just heard. Phil stood there silently for a moment, then sat down across from Tennessee.

"Your 'daughter'? *What* daughter?"

"You...and the others...don't care a hoot about her. She's only a child. You abuse her with your eyes, and your heart. I'll not have it. I'll not have you look at her with lust." He turned his head away.

Phil whispered, "Tennessee, that girl in the magazine is *not* your daughter. I know you. You ain't got no daughter. You told me how when your wife died you were sorry you never had kids."

Tennessee looked over at a confused Phil. "You don't know me. You don't know nothin'. She needs me. It's my job to protect her. I'm going to go find her and tell her how much I love her. She needs me!"

He stood up quickly and, with the magazine clutched tightly in his hand, rushed out of the tavern.

Phil looked over to Artie, hoping for some reassurance that he hadn't finally done it; pushed a harmless old man over the edge. Artie shrugged his shoulders. Gus and Harvey, having witnessed the entire incident, were only concerned about the loss of their magazine.

Suddenly, there was a loud screech of tires outside the tavern. Phil ran outside and everyone else followed.

The driver was already out of his car and standing over the collapsed body of Tennessee.

"He never looked!" the driver shouted. "He ran right out in front of my car and never once looked!"

Artie ran back inside to call for an ambulance, but everyone knew it was probably too late.

Phil took off his jacket and placed it gently over Tennessee's arms and chest. The magazine was still clutched tightly in his hand.

"Damn fool, Tennessee," Gus said out loud to no one in particular.

Phil knelt down to see if Tennessee was still breathing. He was. Tennessee reached up and pulled him closer. He whispered, hoping that only Phil would hear.

" ...I really wanted her to be my daughter," he said.

Harvey turned to Gus. "What did he say?" he asked.

"Something about his daughter," Gus answered.

Phil looked up and wiped away a tear. "He asked me to notify his daughter."

He looked down again just in time to see the old gentleman smile.

# # #

Telephone Madness

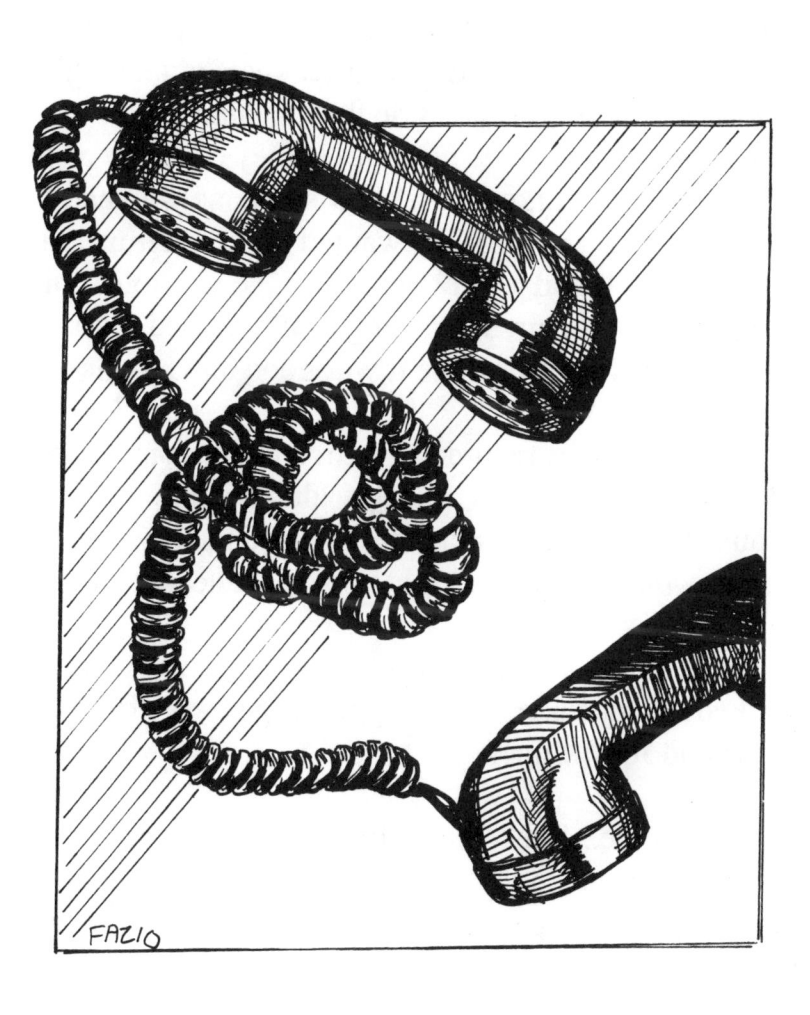

David bought a telephone answering machine long after all of his friends had theirs. Besides the expense — which for David was reason enough not to have one — he never saw the need to screen his calls or record messages when he wasn't home. If he didn't answer they would just call back, he reasoned. But after years of leaving humorous or witty messages on the machines of his friends, he wanted to see how clever they could be on his.

Someone he worked with knew someone who had a friend who had a cousin who wanted to sell their machine pretty cheap. It had a 'problem' once, he was told, but it had since been repaired. As long as it recorded messages and cost less than a new one it was good enough, he thought.

That evening he recorded his first outgoing message: "This is David. But you probably already knew that because you dialed my number. Unfortunately for you, I can't or *won't* talk to you right now. Go ahead, entertain me."

The next day when he returned home, he immediately checked the machine. The only messages were from his best friend Joe Skinner.

BEEP

"Hi, it's me...Joe," the voice said. "When did you get an answering machine? Keeping up with the Skinners, huh? Anyway, I have something very...necessary to talk to you about. Call me when you can."

BEEP

"It's me. Joe, again. Where are you, buddy? I've been waiting for you to call me back. I really need to talk to you. I'll be home for the rest of the night. Call me!"

David dialed Joe's number. The line was busy. In fact, it was busy every time he tried for the rest of the evening. He wondered if maybe he'd gotten the messages wrong. He pressed the Answer button to hear them again. The tape whirred as it rewound. When it reached the beginning it stopped and automatically played back the messages. *Different* messages!

BEEP

"David, it's Joe. I don't know if you can hear me or not, but something weird is going on. I can't explain it. You're going to think I flipped, but do me a favor, will you? Go over to my place and see if I'm there. Don't laugh, just do it. I'll call you back...if I can."

It was some sort of a gag, David figured. Getting even for not returning Joe's calls, he thought. Nevertheless, he grabbed his jacket and hurried over to his friend's apartment — just in case. He had no idea what to expect, but he couldn't help conjuring up thoughts of Joe either passed out on the floor or laughing hysterically on the sofa.

When his knock went unanswered, he used the extra key Joe had given him years ago for emergencies. He called out and searched the apartment but Joe was not there.

"It has to be some kind of a practical joke," David thought.

When he returned home, the red Answer light was flashing on the machine. The message was from his girlfriend.

BEEP

"Hello David, it's Doris. So you went and bought yourself an answering machine. Just as well, I suppose. I have something to tell you and this will make it a lot easier — for me, that is. You'd better sit down. I've thought about us a lot lately, David. I'm sorry, but I...don't think it's working out. I want to start seeing other people. It's nothing personal. It's just that...oh well, let's just leave it at that. That's all I really had to say. If you need to talk, call me. I'll be here. Good-bye, David."

He remained seated as the machine shut itself off with a distinctive click. He was numb. She had caught him totally unaware. As far as he knew, everything was just fine between them. She'd given no prior indication that anything was amiss. Now, she made it perfectly clear. And yet, he wanted to confront her with it. Maybe it was still possible to correct whatever was wrong. But what would he say? He didn't know, but he had to call. He tried her number. It was busy. He then tried calling Joe back. Again, busy. Then Doris — busy.

David rewound the tape and played it back. The message that Doris had left was gone. It was Joe's voice that he heard.

BEEP

"I suppose by now you've gone over to my apartment. I wasn't there, was I? Damn! I had a feeling I wouldn't be. This is weird, David, I mean really *weird*. One minute I'm leaving a message on your machine and the next I...black out or something. I have no memory of what happens after..."

BEEP

"Hello David, this is Doris again. I seem to be having trouble with my phone or maybe it's the phone company. In either case, you are the only one I can reach. Isn't that funny? Since you never called me back I will take that to mean that you are indifferent to our dating other people. That's good, because I have a confession. I've already been seeing someone. For quite some time, as a matter..."

CLICK

David went from being hurt to being angry. How could she do that to him? He was sure that she said what she did just to spite him. He could think of nothing else but to give her a piece of his mind, if only she would get off the damn phone.

He dialed her number — busy. He dialed Joe's number — busy. Could they be talking to each other, he wondered? Not likely, but not impossible either. It wouldn't be the first strange thing that has happened today. First, Joe's wacky, although not very humorous messages, and then the stupid answering machine taking messages before his phone even had a chance to ring! He began to think that he would have been better off paying a little more for a new machine. At least it would have been under warranty. Now, he'd have to bring it in for a cleaning or something and incur the entire repair bill. He hoped that was all that was wrong with it.

The Answer light started blinking. He pressed the button.

BEEP

"David, it's Joe. I think I've figured something out. I know it's going to sound farfetched, but hear me out. I've got to talk fast before your machine beeps me. I don't know how...I don't know why...but the only time I feel like I'm conscious is when I'm leaving you a message. It's like I'm inside your machine. Whatever you do..."

BEEP

"...ah, David? This is Doris, again. Somehow I'm on the phone with you again. I don't even remember calling.

In fact, I draw a blank every time I hang up with you — or your machine, as the case might be. Why don't you call? You don't really care, do you? Then it probably won't bother you to know that the person I've been seeing behind your back is none other than Joe Skinner. That's right, your good friend Joe. He's quite a man, Joe is. He's been able to please me in ways that you never could. Does that bother you, David. It should. We laugh about it all the time. He and I seeing each other, and with you still thinking that I love you. Ha. Like I say, we've gotten quite a laugh..."

BEEP

"David, it's Joe. Please, please whatever you do don't turn your machine off, and don't erase me — I mean my message. Your machine seems to have a mind of it's own, and somehow it's trapped me inside of it. This is no joke. You've got to help me!"

CLICK

David shook his head. These messages weren't funny anymore. Not that they ever were. And if Joe would just get off the phone and not leave so many messages, he would tell him so. But actually there were a few other things he would tell him first. Like the whole business with Doris. He felt betrayed, and it made him mad enough to scream.

The machine was blinking again.

BEEP

"Here I am again, David," Doris said, "although I still don't know how. Remember how I told you that I sort of drew a blank whenever I hung up...like I didn't even exist after that? Well, guess who explained what was happening to me. Someone who has been experiencing the same sensation. That's right — Joe! He's here too!

Wherever 'here' is. This isn't funny, David. If you have something to do with this I am going to be so mad. Joe thinks that if you shut off the machine we may disappear or die or something. I don't believe it, but I do wish you would help us. Whatever you're doing, please stop."

CLICK

David tried calling them both again. Busy. He wondered if...no, it couldn't be possible. But if it was, if the 'souls' of Joe and Doris really were somehow...no, that's madness. Of course, if it *were* true, then he would have absolute power over their existence. What a thought! A less than honest individual in a similar triangle might be tempted to pull the plug on them, so to speak. It was tempting, he had to admit. If anyone deserved it, *they* certainly did. After what they did to him, why should he bother to help them, even if he could?

Out of curiosity, and nothing more, David lifted the faceplate to uncover the control knobs for the machine. As he had suspected, there was a button labeled: Erase. It would be easy, he thought, so easy. He wondered if anyone could possibly trace the erase to him. Could he really push a button and wipe away his girlfriend and his best friend? He corrected himself; his unfaithful former girlfriend and her lover. Yes, he decided, he could.

He placed his finger on the button and pressed. As the tape whirred it emitted a soft, but high pitched, sound. Much like that of a small animal in pain.

When the tape reached the beginning it shut itself off. David immediately pressed Answer. There were no messages.

He then tried calling Joe. The phone was no longer busy. It rang and rang, but no one answered. When he tried calling Doris, her phone also rang and went unanswered. A strange coincidence? He wondered.

The machine was now blinking again. David felt a shiver and didn't want to find out who it was this time. Reluctantly, he pressed Answer.

BEEP

"David? Are you there? This is Mr. Milton from work. Remember work? That's the place where you are required to perform certain duties in the course of a day. A *full* day. We haven't seen much of you lately. Long lunches, short days, and poor performance. You'd better get your butt in gear, boy, or we're going to have a serious conversation, you and I. Do I make myself perfectly..."

BEEP

"David? Milton here. What the hell kind of an answering machine is this? I feel so strange. Like I'm..."

CLICK

David didn't need to think about it this time. He lifted the faceplate, smiled, and wondered how he could get his landlord to call.

# # #

Something's in the Basement

At first, he dismissed it as merely an optical illusion. It wasn't the first time that light reflected off of his eyeglass frame or lens and he misinterpreted it to be an object or someone approaching. Only after it happened a second and third time that day, in the same place, did the 60 year old Alan suspect that something wasn't right.

There in the basement of his suburban home, in the southwest corner of his shop, he saw it again. He turned his head left, and then right, trying to make the ceiling light reflect off his lens. But it was not a reflection of light, or a smudge of dirt, or particles of dust on his lens. There definitely was *something* in that corner.

While sitting on his shop stool, he watched, trying to memorize as many details about it as he could. He would need to, his wife Norma would have a hard time believing it. That is, if she believed it at all. She was not a very understanding or supportive mate.

It was a glittering oval shape, and not very large — perhaps only a yard long, seven or eight inches wide at the middle, and narrowing at the ends. But it was there, hanging in mid-air, unaffected by anything around it. Alan walked around the area. He had to look at it from his peripheral vision, since looking straight at it made it invisible. It wasn't touching anything and it looked the same from all directions.

"Norma!" Alan called from his shop. "Come down here, you won't believe this!"

He began to search the cluttered shop for a pad of paper and a pencil. He'd make a list, he thought. The authorities would want documentation — at least they did on television. He recorded the time of day he saw it, the size, shape, where he was sitting when he first observed it, and in which direction he had to look to see it.

"What are you yelling about?" Norma asked from the top of the stairs.

"Come down here, I want to show you something."

"What is it? Can't you just tell me what it is?" she asked. "I'm watching my show."

She fought him on everything. They'd been married for nine years and they'd not gotten along for the past eight. It was the second marriage for both of them, and they openly admitted to getting married not because they loved each other but simply to avoid loneliness. It wasn't long before they both realized that they had little, if anything, in common. Worse than that, they annoyed each other to no end. He was a retired warehouse worker, and now a full-time tinkerer. She was a full-time television addict with time-out only for the hairdresser or her Monday afternoon bridge game with the neighborhood women. Most days he was left to do his own cooking and laundry because she was too busy with her 'shows.' Marrying Norma was worse than being lonely, he realized.

On any other day Alan would have commented that she was simple-minded, or just plain lazy. But not today. There was something in the basement that he couldn't understand, and he needed a witness.

"Just come down, will you? Do me this!"

By the time Norma reach the shop, Alan was scribbling notes and humming a tune.

"Well? What is this all-important thing that I supposedly won't believe? Make it fast, Dirk is about to find out about Emma's accident."

"Here. Sit here," he said, letting her sit on the shop stool. "Now look straight ahead."

Norma did as he asked and said nothing — as was usually the case whenever she felt he was off on some obscure tangent.

"Okay...," he said, standing back, "out of the corner of your eye, what do you see? In *that* direction off to your left."

He could barely contain his excitement, waiting to share the discovery. *His* discovery.

"What do I 'see'? A cluttered, unkept shop that I've told you a hundred times to clean, is what I see."

Alan shook his head. "Not the shop. Over there by the wall, but not as far as the wall."

Norma turned to look.

"You can't look at it — not directly, at least. You can only see it from the corner of your eye."

Norma looked at him suspiciously. He simply gestured with his hand for her to turn and stare straight ahead.

"*Now* do you see it?"

"I see a stack of old magazines, a vice-thing, the bookcase..."

"No, that's not what I want you to see!" he said loudly, feeling the frustration building up.

"Then *what*?!"

"I don't know what it is, but it's there in the corner. Let me sit down."

Adjusting his glasses, he stared straight ahead. Just as before, the object appeared in his peripheral vision when his head was cocked at a slightly upturned angle.

"It's right there," he said, pointing. "You can't see it?"

"What is it you think you see?" Norma asked.

"It's a...well, I don't know what it is. But it's right there, I can *see* it!" He stood from the stool and showed her where it was. "It's right here!" he said, using both hands to indicate its size. "You can't see it when you look right at it, but from the corner of your eye it looks like a..."

"A what?"

He looked at her. "Like a hole."

She waited for more, but that was all he would offer in the way of explanation. "A hole. In the air. That you can only see when you're not looking at it. Fine. *Now* can I go watch the rest of my show?"

"It's there, I can see it!" he said, looking straight ahead.

"Maybe you're starting to get cardiacs," Norma told him.

"That's 'cataracts,' and no, I am not getting them. I can't see the thing anywhere else except right there and only when my head is turned in such a way."

He was only a year older than she was, but she'd heard of premature senility. Of course, she could never pose that as a possibility, he'd hit the roof. He was always coming up with hairbrained inventions and weird devices to 'make their lives easier.' Like the time he invented a contraption that supposedly would make their car run on water instead of gasoline. The car was in the shop for three weeks getting flushed out.

Another time, he invented a device that sent a small electrical current through their bed springs that was supposed to act as an alarm clock by gently waking them with minor vibrations. The invention never made it past the test run in their basement. The firemen said that if Alan hadn't had a fire extinguisher handy the whole house would have gone up in flames.

"I'll make an appointment so you can get an eye exam. It must be two years since you've seen him. Your prescription probably needs to be changed."

"My eyes are fine," he told her.

"Then you ought to have your head examined. I'm calling your doctor. *Somebody* should look at you. You're having another one of those breakdowns, is what I think. You've flipped. Completely lost it! I think I'll arrange a little time for you down at the lollypop lodge, where everybody else sees things that aren't there, too!"

She was gone before he could argue with her. What did it matter? He knew she wouldn't believe him. She never believed in anything he ever did or tried. All she ever did was tear him down.

His health was fine. And he certainly felt like he had all his faculties. It wasn't his eyes, he thought, or was it? That might explain why he saw this thing and Norma didn't. His eyes, astigmatism and all, looking through a particular prescription lens at a certain angle, allowed him to see...an event, that no one else could see. Maybe it was the combination of these things that made him different and allowed him to see something that wasn't visible to others. Yes, that's what it had to be.

Alan spent the remainder of the evening and early morning hours observing the 'hole' and noting things about it. Moving sideways toward it, he could see it more clearly. It was indeed a hole. A hole that, as far as he knew, didn't exist yesterday. He felt he had to conduct experiments.

For the first experiment, he took a flashlight and slowly panned a beam of light across the room. The light broke as it passed the hole. That meant that *something* was there, he reasoned.

Next, still sitting sideways in order to see it, he lobbed a wadded piece of paper toward the opening. It disappeared silently. He searched the floor, the workbench, and the bookcase before convincing himself that the paper ball had indeed entered the hole.

The desire to know all there was to know of the hole was insatiable, and it pushed him onward. Cautiously, he reached toward the hole. His hand trembled slightly, not knowing what it would feel like or what was on the other side, yet it was a risk he felt he had to take for the sake of science.

His fingers slowly entered the hole. It felt cool.

"Alan!" Norma shouted from the top of the stairs.

Startled, he immediately yanked his hand away from the hole and began rubbing his fingers. "Yes?!" he called, relieved she'd interrupted when she had.

"It's two o'clock in the morning! You're not still feeding your delusion are you? When are you coming to bed?!"

Alan looked at his watch. He'd been so involved with the discovery that he'd lost all track of time. He'd done all he could — it was time to call it a night.

Early the next morning, Alan immediately went to the basement. He wanted to see if the hole was still there, or if it had moved, or if he'd just been imagining the whole thing. It couldn't have been a dream, he thought, he remembered all too well the coolness on his fingers.

It was still there. Right where it first appeared. But it seemed different in some way. Sitting sideways, he used a yardstick to measure the opening. The width was almost the same, but today it measured only twenty-four inches long — twelve inches shorter than yesterday! The hole was closing.

"Are you down there *again*?!" Norma called from the top of the stairs.

"Yes, I'm down here again!" he answered.

"Cleaning up, I hope. You'd better be cleaning up. I've told you a hundred times to clean up that damn shop. How many times do I have to..."

"The hole is closing," he called up to her, disappointingly.

"The one in your head? You're not still waving at the air, are you?"

"It's some kind of atmospheric phenomenon. A tear in the universe. Or a chance encounter with a universe in another dimension." He thought about that for a moment. "Yes...a parallel universe. Maybe a link with another world, and *I* found it!"

"Just 'find' the broom and start cleaning up down there! I'm tired of all your goofy projects that never work. You spend too much time down there. Are you listening, Alan? You only think about yourself. You're a loser. You'll always be a loser. Why don't you do something constructive instead of wasting your time with your loser projects. Are you listening to a word I'm saying?!"

Alan measured the opening again. It was only twenty-three inches long. The rate of closure was increasing — he had to act fast.

For the entire length of their marriage she had nagged, complained, and criticized him to death. 'You're stupid,' she would say. 'A putz. You don't ever do anything *I* want. You're selfish, childish, and can't even pick up after yourself! You're a loser,' she insisted, almost on a daily basis. 'A loser!'

Enough, he thought. Her day had finally come.

Although the thoughts of leaving her or throwing her out crossed his mind only on particularly bad days, he never seriously considered either. He had gone through one messy divorce, he didn't want to go through another. Of course, murder was out of the question. The chances of a person getting away with murder were slim, he reasoned, unless, of course, they had an airtight alibi, or could make the victim disappear into thin air. Thanks to his new found discovery, Alan knew he could have both.

It was a one in a billion opportunity, he thought, and one he couldn't pass up. While Norma was engrossed watching her favorite morning television programs in the kitchen, Alan secretly slipped a small amount of antifreeze into her tea. After serving her, he went back to the basement and waited. Thirty minutes later, he heard a loud thud. When he returned to the kitchen, Norma was laying dead on the floor.

"I think you're right, Norma," he said, as he dragged her down the stairs to his shop. "I've been putting things off much too long. It's about time I start cleaning up around here."

Within an hour, Norma was a pile of ten individually wrapped white packages. One by one the packages were pushed through the hole. Soon after, the hole completely disappeared.

Moments later in a house on the opposite side of town, a young boy woke his father.

"Daddy, wake up. Wake up, Daddy!"

"Wha...what's wrong?" he asked, half asleep.

"Is it Christmas?" the boy asked.

"Christmas? No, it's not Christmas."

The boy held up the arm-long present neatly wrapped in white freezer paper, tied securely with twine. "Can I keep it, Daddy? Can I? Is this one mine?"

The boy's father rubbed his eyes and looked at the package his son held. "What's that? Where did you get it?"

"In the basement," the boy answered. "I was playing with the train and then I seen them."

"The basement? Where in the basement?"

"It was in the corner," he answered. "With a bunch of other ones. They weren't there yesterday, that's how I know it's Christmas!"

"Maybe Mommy wants to surprise us," his father said, taking the package. "While she's at church let's take a peek. Go get the scissors off the kitchen table. But be careful, they're sharp."

He rose from the bed, donned his robe, and eagerly awaited his son's return. They both loved surprises.

# # #

Brother Edwin

"Be still my brother," Louis told him, "it shan't be much longer."

He closed the solid oak door to Edwin's room, drew the bolt, and carefully applied the padlock. He had lied, as he had so many times over the past year, but only God knew how long it would be before a housemaid would be hired. A *suitable* housemaid, that is. One that not only was qualified, but could also be trusted to keep their secret.

Louis loved his brother, but it seemed a lifetime ago that he was free to live his own life. Not since their mother's death five years ago had he been able to live any type of normal existence. Since then, he has been a slave to the estate and, of course, keeper of his brother.

Edwin had been in good care with their mother; not only out of motherly love, Louis decided, but also out of the extreme guilt she felt for the accident. She was not responsible, and Louis held no animosity toward her, but after it happened she was never quite right.

If blame was to be placed anywhere, it should be with their father, Louis believed. He was the one who moved them to that desolate estate miles outside the nearest town, deep in the woods. No telephone, no newspaper, no television...nothing to link them with the rest of humanity. All because he wanted to get away from the rat race he faced five days a week at his job. It was ironic, Louis thought. His father moved from the city to be alone, yet *he* would give anything *not* to be.

After Father died unexpectedly, Mother did her best to raise the two boys alone. Maintaining the six bedroom estate on fifty acres of wooded property was an overwhelming responsibility in itself, and quite expensive. But Father had built up a hefty nest egg through stock options and business acquisitions, so his family was left fairly well-off. Hired help ran the estate while Mother ran the hired help.

The loss of her husband and the sudden responsibility of raising two young children while maintaining an estate proved to be an enormous burden for her. She began to drink to soften the depression, often in the middle of the afternoon. She laid out the day's agenda for the staff and then they rarely saw her again until the next day. She was usually in her room or the study, drinking or crying or both.

She was in favor of liquidating the estate and moving back to the city, and probably would have if Edwin hadn't wandered into the woods that fateful night. He was only seven; impulsive and headstrong. He'd been taught not to wander away from the house — regardless of the time of day, but he felt like a walk that night so he took it.

The staff had all gone home for the night and the house was quiet and peaceful. Edwin had been gone for a half hour before Mother realized that he was not around. Moments after she noticed he was missing, the screams began. Bloodcurdling, flesh-crawling screams.

"Oh my God!" Louis remembered his mother yelling, as she ran out of the house and into the woods. "My baby! My baby!"

Louis, then twelve, ran close behind, but thought enough to grab a flashlight and baseball bat on the way out.

The screams continued for a few moments more, then ended.

"Edwin! Edwin!" Mother called as she ran. Then she stopped.

The beam from the flashlight fell on Edwin, lying on the path, unconscious. His clothes were shredded and bloodsoaked. His face, arms, and legs had been bitten and gnawed so badly he was barely recognizable.

Louis dropped the flashlight and doubled over with nausea. Mother knelt beside Edwin, weeping, and nearly hysterical, looking for any sign of life. "He's still alive...," she said through her tears, "he's alive! Give me the flashlight!"

Louis did as he was told. As he passed the flashlight to her, the beam landed on a figure twenty feet away. A large wolf was up ahead on the path, waiting, and watching with eyes that glowed in the light. It growled when the light hit it. As Mother panned the light, they could see another wolf in the brush. And another. And another.

Edwin had stumbled upon a wolf's den, they reasoned. But for the grace of God he was still alive. The question was...for how long?

"Louis, we've got to get Edwin home. Be still my son," she said, as she wrapped her young son in her sweater. "I'll get you home and you'll be all right. I promise. Nothing will ever happen to you again. I promise!"

The wolves growled, almost in unison. It was their dinner she was about to take away and they would not have it. Louis heard them inching closer, and knew that there was only one way to save his brother. As nervous as he was, he let out the loudest yell he could and started swinging wildly at them with the bat. They moved backwards into the brush.

Mother cradled Edwin in her arms and ran back down the path. When the wolves were far enough away, Louis quickly followed his mother.

They both knew that Edwin needed medical attention. But the estate didn't have a telephone, and the doctor was too far away to be reached in time. Fortunately, Mother had taken first aid before she married, and was able to keep him alive. Even then, Louis suspected that it was a mistake.

Mother planned to tend to him until the morning and, after his condition stabilized, drive him into town to see the doctor. It didn't quite work out that way.

By the next morning, she had convinced herself that she had been horribly negligent as a mother and was determined that news of Edwin would never leave the estate. Although he still had not regained consciousness, Edwin seemed stable. By then, however, Mother was too ashamed to bring him into town. She immediately dismissed the entire servant staff so that no one would know of the accident.

As the days passed, Louis could tell that his mother was changing. The accident had made her neurotic and extremely protective. Louis was forbidden to leave the house except to do the chores. He was not allowed to go to school or go into town for any reason. Twice a month Mother drove into town alone and bought supplies and groceries.

One positive thing that came from the accident was that she'd stopped drinking. She had to. She was with Edwin almost constantly, day after day, tending to his wounds, and she felt that she needed her wits about her. Her outpouring of care and love would bring him back to health, she reasoned. She was wrong.

It was nearly three weeks before he regained consciousness. His small body was nearly all covered with scabs and bandages. Whether it was from pain, or the shock of the attack, Edwin wailed as he woke.

His vocal cords had been irreparably damaged by the wolves and he was never able to speak again. Any utterances at all were grunts, whimpers, coos, and cries. He made these sounds whenever he tried to communicate. At first, it was difficult understanding what he wanted. But just as an infant makes different sounds to attract attention, so did Edwin. They soon learned what each sound meant and they thought nothing of answering to a grunt or a moan.

Edwin never did completely return to health, in spite of Mother's attention and dedication. His body was badly damaged and disfigured. His face was hideously altered. Mother didn't seem to notice, or at least pretended not to. He was her son, her baby, and she could not, or would not, see the truth.

Louis found himself adopting a fatherly role to Edwin. But it was an incredible responsibility caring for his recuperating brother, and he found himself constantly stressed and exhausted. Why Edwin didn't die in the woods that night, Louis didn't know. Perhaps he should have, Louis thought many times to himself. It broke his heart to see his brother that way.

Louis grew up fast doing the chores normally done by the staff. Keeping the thirteen room house fairly clean was an all-day job. Weekends were entirely devoted to landscape.

Mother had returned to drinking heavily in an effort to cope, and was no help at all with the chores. Louis knew his time was no longer his own. He felt that in many ways he'd become a prisoner. Every day while he was maintaining an estate he didn't want to live in, he wondered if that would be the day that his brother would die. Sadly, only then would he and his mother be free to sell the estate, move to the city, and attempt to lead normal lives again. But Edwin held on...year after year.

The years passed slowly for Louis; tending to the house and property. As he grew older, his resentment grew as well, although he could never quite pinpoint who or what he was resentful toward. Whether it was his mother, Edwin, his father, God, or himself, there were reasons attributable to each.

His least favorite chores of his day were to clean and feed Edwin. Fortunately, he had to do that only when Mother took ill. Unfortunately, Mother's alcoholic binges were getting worse, and Louis had to be Edwin's primary carekeeper more often than he or his brother would have liked.

Edwin's body was so badly deformed that he looked nothing like the little boy Louis had loved playing with. His spinal cord had been damaged so severely it was years before he could leave the bed. And even then, he was only able to move by crawling on his hands and knees. He looked, acted, and sounded like some sort of animal, but his eyes...his eyes were all that was left of the Edwin that Louis remembered. There was a certain sparkle left that conveyed, "I know you are my brother...don't forget me."

As Edwin got older and stronger, his sixteen year old body and mannerisms remained grotesque and animal in form. His hair grew long and unkept. What facial hair he had went unshaven. His fingernails and toenails went untrimmed. At night he would curl up and sleep in the corner of his room. During the day he would pace on all fours. Louis wondered whether his mother still felt that she could 'reach' him. It was getting harder for Louis to work up the courage to even try.

Edwin was going through more than physical changes. The constant pain, discomfort, and loneliness, must have been unbearable for him, for sometimes late at night, long after Louis and his mother had retired, Edwin would cry. Long, wailing, mournful howls that would send shivers down Louis's spine. Many nights they kept Louis awake, and often made him cry, too. God should take him, Louis would think. Why doesn't God take him?

Mother's depression got progressively worse over the years, and she rarely left her own room. Louis now had to do all of the cooking, cleaning, and feeding of his brother. This meant having even less time to spend on the landscape. Slowly, nature began to win the outdoor battle. Bushes went untrimmed, the lawn went uncut, and the weeds won out over the flowers.

By the time Mother died, Edwin was twenty years old and totally dependent on Louis for everything. He ate when Louis brought food, and was clean only when Louis would clean him. It was quite different than when Mother was in charge. Then, she would spend all day with him. Talking with him, cleaning him, feeding him...all out of love. But after thirteen years, Edwin had become just another chore for Louis. And an unpleasant one at that. He was fed twice a day and cleaned every two days. His bedroom and bathroom were cleaned once a week. Many times Edwin wouldn't even use the toilet to relieve himself. The smell of the room was pungent, and Louis dreaded having to enter.

Edwin had always been relatively calm and restrained

under the constant watch of his mother. But extreme loneliness and incapacitation grew to be an overwhelming burden without his mother there to soothe and console him. Louis was not nearly as generous or patient as his mother. Louis did his chores and left Edwin alone, spending no more time with him than was necessary.

As time passed, Edwin grew restless waiting for his brother to come around. Day after day he would pace on his hands and knees like a caged animal. Sometimes he would claw at the door for hours. His calm disposition changed dramatically. Hope had turned to anger, and anger turned to fury. In occasional fits of rage, Edwin would even throw his furniture around the room.

Louis was sure his brother was becoming uncontrollably insane. He removed almost everything from the room, leaving only a mattress, some blankets, and a pile of old magazines. He began to worry about his own safety, and made less frequent trips to the room.

Random screams tore the night and kept him awake. Growls and clawing sounds began coming from the room at all hours of the day. Louis considered institutionalization, but couldn't bring himself to do it — either because of a deep-seated caring, or fear of chastisement for not having done it sooner.

Something needed to be done, however, so Louis decided to hire someone to help him with Edwin. Someone who could be trusted to keep silent about what they saw. Someone who would not be repulsed at helping this...man, who was physically and mentally unable to help himself. Someone who would not be afraid.

A drifter chanced upon the estate one day, looking for a dry place to bed down.

"I thought the place was deserted," he told Louis, who surprised him at the door. "It didn't look like anyone's lived here for years, no offense."

"That's all right, I understand," Louis told him. "My brother has been...ill, and it's kept me from my other chores. I'm looking for help, if you're interested in employment."

The middle aged man thought for a moment. "Sure," he said. "I got no place to go, and no money to get there. Why not?"

"Very well," Louis said. "Do you have family, friends, that you need to contact to tell them you'll be staying?"

The man shook his head. "Nobody."

Louis put the man to work immediately, cleaning and straightening. He put off sending the man in to see Edwin until that evening for fear of scaring him off.

When dinner was made, Louis put it all on a tray and gave it to the man. "Come, let's introduce you to my brother. Edwin had an accident as a child," Louis explained on the way to the room, "so he's not quite...right. But I think you'll get along just fine."

Louis unlocked the door and held it open for the man to enter. Edwin was sitting on the floor against the wall, hunched over and looking at the pictures in a magazine.

"Ah...howdy buddy," the man began to say. "I'm going to be..."

He'd only taken one step further when Edwin suddenly rushed at him. After knocking the tray to the floor, Edwin pulled the man down and began pummeling him repeatedly with his fists. He then began to bite feverishly at the man's throat.

"Edwin!" Louis shouted. "Edwin! Stop!"

But it was no use. Edwin had gone completely insane. He was more animal than human at that moment.

Screams permeated the house. For fear of his own life, Louis ran out of the room and slammed the door behind him. With his back against the door he held his ears until the screams stopped.

Cautiously, he opened the door. Edwin was sitting on the dead man's chest eating the food that had fallen from the tray. He seemed calmer than he had in months.

Edwin tilted his head, "Hmm... ," he moaned gently, as if thanking his brother.

It was fortunate, Louis thought, that the man had no family, no friends...no one who would miss him. Louis buried the drifter a few hundred feet from the house in the middle of the woods. It upset him greatly, but he had to admit the incident had calmed Edwin down, there was no doubt about it. For weeks afterwards he seemed content to just stare out the window or look at the pictures in his magazines. When it came time for feeding or cleaning, he was much more patient and relaxed. It had been the outlet for his aggression and he'd gotten it out of his system. Or so it seemed.

As the months passed, Edwin was once again getting restless and uncooperative. He howled at night and began to growl as Louis brought food or magazines. It had been a year since the incident with the drifter and once again Louis was afraid to enter his brother's room for any reason.

Louis had just locked Edwin's room for the night when he heard the door knocker pound the front door. He opened the door and greeted the young woman standing there holding a newspaper.

"You must be here in response to my advertisement for a housemaid," Louis said.

"Yes. I would have been here earlier, but I had a heck of a time finding you."

"Yes," Louis said, smiling, "we're a bit off the beaten path. But you shouldn't have traveled at night, it could be dangerous. Someone you care about may be concerned."

She looked at him, confused. "Oh, no. There's no one. My parents died years ago. There's just little old me. I'm trying to earn money to go to Europe — to start over. I look after myself now." She laughed.

Louis smiled. "That's fine. Fine. Come, let's introduce you to my brother. He had an accident as a child, so he's not quite...right. But I think he'll like you just fine."

# # #

Clementine's Yard

No one liked talking about the bizarre disappearance of Clementine's young daughter, it was just a sad and unfortunate event that happened. The incident made all the newspapers, and there was a nationwide search, but she was never found. For a while it transformed this quaint little town into a paranoid media circus.

Things settled down as the years passed. The police closed the case file and concluded that she was 'missing, presumed dead.' Some of the townspeople moved on and others locked their doors, whereas they hadn't before, but the town really never changed that much.

Meanwhile, lives were lived, children grew up and had children, and people found other things to talk about other than a past blemish on their town. Oh, the subject may have surfaced occasionally in the barbershop, or some other unlikely place, but for the most part, the adults rarely spoke of it at all. It was, however, a favorite subject among the children. And their fascination for the supernatural always seemed to peak at this time of the year — late summer — for that was when 'it' happened. And today was the exact day.

The townspeople of Moosehart went about their business in the usual way; groceries were purchased, fences were mended, lumber was cut, and diapers were changed. No one gave the day any special significance. Two twelve year old boys sitting in their school cafeteria thought differently.

"Jimmy Duesser told me that *he* jumped over the fence last year and was there almost all night!" Roy said.

"And he never got caught?" Skip asked.

"No. He never did."

"Well...? What did he see?" Skip asked, expecting to hear a graphic description of haunting spirits, stalking zombies, or bloodcurdling screams.

Roy took his time before answering. He knew he had Skip's full attention. One by one he cracked each knuckle on both of his hands. It calmed him down. It drove Skip crazy.

"He didn't see nothin'," he said finally. "No Clementine, no daughter, no nothin'."

Skip sat back in his chair and sighed. "He didn't see nothin'."

Roy looked around at the nearby tables to see if anything they had said had been overheard. This was not a subject either of them wanted spread around. Not yet, anyway. No one was looking so he continued.

"Look, there's a lot of reasons why we gotta do it. Forty years ago she got croaked. And every year on that date, she comes back and somebody sees her. This year it's gonna be us. And besides, Duesser is always bragging his head off about some stupid little thing, isn't he? Well, he ain't bragging about *that*!"

Skip shrugged his shoulders. "What's there to brag about, he didn't see nothin'."

"Maybe not. But don't you figure he'd at least brag that he *did* it?" Roy asked.

"I don't know, maybe...," Skip answered.

"I thinks he knows something!"

Skip stared at his friend, ignoring his lunch for a moment. "What could he 'know'? He didn't *see* nothin'!"

Roy whispered, "I think he seen one of 'em and is just too scared to tell anybody what he saw."

"So who cares?" Skip said under his breath. He then turned his attention to the sandwich that he brought from home. His interest in Clementine was dissipating quickly.

"*I* care. And *you* should too!" Roy answered. "Somebody has to stay in the cemetery long enough to see what there is to see. See?" Roy laughed and finished his milk.

"You're nuts."

"And you're a *chicken*!" Roy said. He crushed the milk carton in his hands.

"I am *not* a chicken," Skip defended. "And I still think you're nuts."

"Look, it'll be easy, really. Hardly nobody ever goes down there. Until they die, of course!" He laughed. "Another reason we gotta do it is that nobody *ever* spent the night. We'll be heroes! The girls will think we're cooler than the eighth graders!"

Skip's head popped to attention and his eyes lit up for the first time since they started talking about the whole idea. Heroes? Admiration from the girls? That alone might be worth the risk of a confrontation with Clementine or his dead daughter, Skip thought.

"I'll be dead if my old man catches me!"

"You sneak out. Tell them you're going to bed, open your window, crawl down the gutter and you're out. Just like you was comin' over to my house. You've done it before."

"That was different."

He *had* done it before. Just two weeks ago, as a matter of fact. And many times before that. He would sneak over to Roy's house late in the evening after their parents went to sleep, and they would play a game or read comic books. Each time that he snuck out held an element of excitement and danger, but the risk was mostly that of getting caught by his parents. He was either very lucky or very quiet because his midnight runs were never discovered. This time would be different, however. This time there was the danger of unspeakable horror that might be encountered in a dark cemetery in the middle of the night.

"You're scared," Roy insisted.

"I ain't!"

Roy smiled.

Fellow classmate Chuckie Melville came over to their table. "What's new?" he asked.

"Me and Skip are going to spend the night in Clementine's Cemetery!" Roy boasted.

Skip was surprised that Roy blurted it out as he had. He'd let the cat out of the bag! Skip knew that once Chuckie knew, word would spread like wildfire. He had to admit to himself, however, that it was somewhat exciting to think that half the school would soon know what their plan was. It was almost as good as doing the act itself. Almost. The downside was that now there was no way to back away from the challenge. To do so would surely brand them both as cowards. To a twelve year old, that was *worse* than death.

"No kidding?! You guys are really going over there? For the *whole* night?"

He was understandably excited. They were the closest friends he knew that would even attempt it. Except, of course, for Jimmy Duesser, who no one believed anyway.

Skip looked up and saw the excitement on Chuckie's face. Roy was sitting back in his chair, smiling, with his arms crossed. He knew then that it was decided.

"When are you guys doing it?"

Roy refused to let his eyes meet Skip's.

"We were just talking about it now," Skip said, staring directly at his partner.

Chuckie wished both of them good luck, grinned, and hurried off to his next class. They sat in silence for a moment.

"Then it's settled," Roy said at last.

"I still think it's the stupidest thing I ever heard."

"You're just a chicken."

"I *ain't* chicken!" Skip insisted.

"Anyway, you're in it, whether you want to be or not. Once Chuckie opens his mouth the whole school will know. It's up to you now. You can go along and be a hero, or stay home and tomorrow you can tell everybody that you were too scared."

Skip looked down and saw that his milk carton had been crushed. Again, Roy was smiling.

They were to face Clementine and his daughter that very night, on the anniversary of her death, when it was almost certain that she would reappear — or so went the legend.

All through dinner, Skip ran the list of preparations through his head. Flashlight, pocket knife, burnt cork — to camouflage his face and hands from evil spirits — and a candy bar in case it was a long night.

When the time came, he wanted to be ready, physically and mentally, but his mind wandered. It often did when under the pressure of a late homework assignment or having to face his father after misbehaving. This time it was only slightly different. This time he knew he had even less time to prepare himself.

During dinner, he pushed his vegetables from one side of the plate to the other. His mind was cluttered with stories, rumors, and fears. He had heard most every version of Old Man Clementine's life since he was old enough to listen. The most common one was that Clementine's seven year old daughter had wandered away from the house many years ago and was killed by a spirit which roamed the cemetery next door to their house.

As legend had it, Clementine, the caretaker of the only cemetery in Moosehart County, then declared war on all evil spirits and stalked the graveyard at midnight every year on the anniversary of his daughter's death hoping to catch evil spirits loitering where normal spirits lay in peace.

All the children in town knew that an old man who lived alone next to a cemetery at the edge of town with no wife and a dead kid killed by spirits, was better off left alone. Usually, the children walked on the other side of the street.

"Anything interesting happen at school, Skipper?" his father asked that night over dinner.

Skip immediately looked up after quickly flattening the miniature tombstone he'd sculptured out of mashed potatoes. His father rarely asked about school. He usually talked about the lumberyard, or putting a new roof on the barn, or some other boring adult stuff. Strange that he should ask about school on that particular evening, Skip thought.

"Skipper?" asked his mother, "are you paying attention?"

"Nothing!" he answered.

"Classes okay?" his father asked.

"Fine," he said, thinking that he'd better come up with some news to avoid suspicion. "Marianne Brewster is going to flunk English."

After he said it, he was sorry he had. Out of all the trivial news he could have shared, why did he choose Marianne? She lived closest to the Clementine place, and all it would take would be to have his father mention Clementine's name. The guilt would surely be written all over Skip's face.

He had never really considered himself to be a dishonest kid, but to try and keep a secret the magnitude of stalking Clementine's property was nearly as bad as an out-and-out lie. Not being a good liar, Skip's father almost always caught him whenever he tried. He knew he couldn't get caught *this* time, there would be a tanning in it for sure.

He wondered if fathers could read minds. That certainly would explain the persistent school-related questions. He couldn't be sure, but he wasn't willing to take any chances. He tried to think of anything other than the cemetery. It was hard. The Clementine stories had been a part of the heritage of Moosehart County for as long as anyone could remember. The more he strained to think of something else, the more his mind seemed to drift back to the cemetery.

He began to feel tiny beads of perspiration accumulate on his brow. He had to be careful, for if his mother thought he was sick, she would keep an especially close eye on him all night and he would be trapped. He was lucky, she didn't notice his brow.

"That's a shame about Marianne," his father said. Not that interested in Marianne Brewster's command of the English language, his father redirected the conversation. "Bobbie Allison is with child from a boy in Middleton," he said.

Whew! That was adult enough for him to daydream of

other things without drawing suspicion. What luck!

After dinner, Skip waited until it was late enough to say he was going to bed. He especially did not want extra attention tonight. At nine-thirty it was time. He usually went to bed at ten o'clock, but it wouldn't be noticed, and he couldn't wait any longer.

He said goodnight to his parents, went up to his room, and changed clothes. He stuffed his pockets with all the things he needed to bring, careful not to crush the candy bar. He replaced the tee-shirt he had been wearing with a dark blue sweatshirt. He didn't have black. Roy said to wear black so that neither Clementine nor the evil spirits would see them. It would mean torturous things if either one did.

He took special care with tying the laces of his sneakers. If he had to leave the cemetery in a hurry, he did not want to be slowed by shoes with loose laces. They would surely cause him to trip and fall into the clutches of Old Man Clementine...or worse. Again, Roy's suggestion. He darkened his face and hands with the burnt cork and tested the flashlight.

Lastly, there had to be a note. Just in case.

'Dear Mom and Dad,

If you are reading this, I must be killed.
It was probably Old Man Clementine that done killed me. Roy is probably killed too.
Please don't be mad.

love,
Your son, Skip Monroe'

He folded the letter in half and propped it up against his pillow. With that, he slowly looked around the room, perhaps he thought, for the last time. All of his favorite items were within view: a football helmet, his skateboard, a baseball mitt, and a half dozen various baseball cards scattered on his desk. They would all be left behind, just waiting for him to return — he hoped.

He was ready, it was all memorized. Slowly, he opened the window and carefully scurried along the downspout, as he had done so many times before. Only this time, he made it a point not to look back.

"What do you think he'll do when he realizes that Roy isn't coming?" Mrs. Monroe asked her husband, as she lay in bed with the novel she was trying to finish.

He set his magazine on the nightstand and took off his reading glasses. "The same thing *I* did when *my* 'partner' never showed up...spend the night alone."

"It was very nice of Roy's parents to call and tell us," she said. "If Roy hadn't confessed, we might never have known."

"Yes. Very nice," Mr. Monroe repeated.

"What about Mr. Clementine?" she asked.

"Bill? He'll keep his eye on Skip. Seems like every year some fool kid has to go and prove to himself that nothing's going to happen."

She reached over and turned off the lamp. "And tonight it's my baby."

"Tonight it's my son," he said.

# # #

The Last Alternative

They were both devout Catholics. Divorce was out of the question. But it had been a year since they shared a meaningful conversation; months since they had felt comfortable together. He had begun to wonder if divorce wasn't the only viable solution left.

They had talked with friends about their marital problems, but it didn't help. Jack's friends supported *him*, of course, while Lisa's friends supported her. Nobody really offered any advice they could use.

They spoke with her parents, who always seemed to have the answer to everything, but their only advice was, 'Work it out.'

They tried seeing a professional marriage counselor with lukewarm results. On three separate occasions they met with the counselor, but they felt that the meetings were nothing more than gripe sessions and hardly worth their time.

Lisa even suggested a marriage reconciliation group that met for a weekend at a lodge fifty miles away to try and work it out. As a group, they discussed various solutions to typical marital confrontations. It was surprising to hear that so many couples had so many problems.

Unfortunately, none of the remedies drew them any closer. In fact, in a way, each attempt just seemed to frustrate them and push them further apart. It was no surprise that Jack was skeptical of Lisa's latest plan. It would be the last one, he thought to himself. After that...who knows.

He thought he still loved her, especially her undaunted

optimism, but it was as if they had little left in common other than a pair of matching gold wedding bands. It just didn't seem to be enough to hold a marriage together.

Jack worked in the credit department of a large corporation. His days were filled by calling customers who were delinquent in their accounts. Conversations often turned heated. He was sympathetic to many of them, of course, but it was his job to insist that they pay the balance owed as quickly as possible. "Squeezing blood out of a turnip," was how he described it. It was not how he thought he would earn his living when he took all those business management classes in college, but it paid the bills. It left him feeling drained and mentally exhausted by the end of the day.

Lisa always asked him how his day was and what happened at the office, but Jack didn't like to talk about it. When he got home, the furthest thing from his mind was talking about a dead-end job where he had to threaten people all day. Lisa could never understand how difficult it was for him to open up after a day like that.

Lisa was just the opposite. She was a social service coordinator at the Center for the Handicapped. It was a high-pressure position that she'd held for the past four years. There wasn't much salary to speak of, but there was a good opportunity for advancement. Plus, it brought her a great deal of joy to help those less fortunate than herself. When she got home, she wanted to share all the experiences of her day, even the unpleasant ones. Venting the pressures of the day always relieved her tension. Unfortunately, when Jack got home he was never in the mood to talk or be talked to — especially about unpleasant events. Subsequently, they hardly talked at all.

They rarely argued, but faced evening after evening of near silence. The pressure of their careers had taken its toll on their relationship to the point where they both felt they were strangers living in the same house.

Neither Jack nor Lisa were eager to abandon what they'd spent the last seven years building, but casual mention of separation was cropping up into what little conversation they still had. With the fear of an imminent divorce, he agreed to her suggestion.

Before Lisa left for her mother's house, she wrote a note that Jack found when he got home from work. It briefly inventoried the contents of the refrigerator and freezer. There was more than enough food for the few days that she would be gone. He wadded the note with a smile and left it lying on the table.

Jack prepared himself for the evening. He shaved, showered, and splashed on his favorite cologne. As he stood in front of the closet, he spent nearly ten minutes choosing a tie. At first, he chose one that Lisa had given him, but then replaced it with one he had bought before they were married. At last he was ready.

Before he left, he twisted off his wedding band and left it on the dresser top. The missing ring left a whitish circle around his finger, but it wouldn't be noticed in a dimly lit lounge, he thought.

It only took twenty minutes to drive over to the Riverside Lounge on Mulhullen Drive, but it seemed much longer. He wasn't sure if he felt embarrassed or excited, but knew that one of those feelings would prevail by the end of the evening.

The lounge was starting to fill up on this Friday evening, but there were still a few empty stools at the bar. Although he hadn't been there since he and Lisa first met, it still looked the same. The booths were shaped like dockside shipping cartons with large fishnets covering the walls and ceiling. Shells, fishing lures, and floats of various sizes were tangled in the netting.

He sat at the far end of the L-shaped bar, where he always sat with his friends when he was single. It provided a clear view of the entire lounge.

By ten o'clock, and two drinks later, he began to wonder if it was a good idea for him to be there. Then she strolled in. Her long, normally straight, brown hair had been restyled with loose flowing curls, while the black cotton dress that she wore clung to her body in a most seductive way.

Glancing casually around the lounge, Lisa sat at the opposite end of the bar. He had never seen her wearing that dress before and had to admit that she looked stunning in it.

He finished his drink and awaited the refill. In the time it took the bartender to refill his glass, a handsome young man Jack's age approached her. Jack couldn't tell what they were saying, but he assumed they were introducing themselves. At any moment she would ask the man to leave, Jack figured, and he would take his rightful place beside her to start the game. Instead, she smiled and the man sat down next to her.

How inconsiderate she was to be smiling and chatting with a total stranger while her husband fumed at the end of the bar, he thought. How dumb he was to be talked into doing this in the first place! This was *not* the way to straighten out a marriage.

An hour passed and she still had not asked the intruder to leave. Jack grew annoyed at her lack of compassion and wanted to grab her by the hand and take her home. Either that, or rough up her new friend. He no longer wanted any part of her infantile marriage remedies.

Another drink was ordered. Still, she sat there talking and smiling.

"Bust his face," Jack thought. "I'll walk right over and bop him in his interfering nose."

No, wait. The subtle approach was better, he reasoned. He called over the bartender and sent a drink to "the young lady at the other end of the bar." At last this would break the ice, he hoped. He smiled when she received it and looked over, but to his amazement she declined the drink.

"That's it!" he thought, "I'm leaving! I'm gonna walk right past her and go home!"

Unfortunately, he knew he couldn't leave his wife sitting at a bar flirting with another man. That would be asking too much of his pride.

Just when he started feeling like he had lost her completely, the guy she had been talking to got up and walked further down the bar to introduce himself to an attractive blond that had come in about thirty minutes earlier. Lisa sat alone for the first time that evening and nursed the last of her drink.

Not wishing to lose out on another opportunity to talk with her, Jack carried his drink over to where she was sitting. "May I join you?" he asked.

"If you like," she answered.

He said nothing for several minutes. "Why didn't you take the drink I sent over?"

She glanced over to him. "I don't accept drinks from strangers."

Of course. She was playacting. At least, he hoped so.

He drew a deep breath. He felt stupid playing this silly game. This would be the last one, he promised himself.

"Would you mind if I bought you one if I introduce

myself?" She looked over at him and he continued. "I'm Jack. I was sitting down the bar there and I noticed you as soon as you came in."

"How many times have you used *that* line before?" she asked.

"I thought I'd like to meet you, that's all. I'm not good at starting conversations, so it's hard for me to meet nice people. And sometimes even after I've met someone nice, I have a tough time opening up. But conversation *is* important, don't you think?"

She nodded. "Yes, I do."

"You seem to be a nice person, and I didn't want you to walk in and out of my life without telling you."

The words flowed from his lips just as they had when he first said them to her on the night they met.

"I'm Lisa," she said, as she extended her hand.

He reached out and shook it.

They stared into each others eyes and smiled. He no longer cared that she'd been flirting with a complete stranger. If it was part of the act to get him jealous, then it worked and he didn't care. All he knew was that he was feeling something for her that he'd forgotten he'd *ever* felt. He knew that they would still have some problems, but he wanted her in his life and hoped that she felt the same way.

"Lisa, the very first time we ever sat in this lounge together I was madly infatuated with you. I still am."

She place her hand on top of his. "Yes, I think I *will* let you buy me that drink."

Unlike their first meeting, he didn't need to ask. This time he knew she would let him serve it at home.

# # #

The Big "L"
(A Play on Love)

A 3-scene play with one stage setting: the dining room of one family's house. A large oval dining room table is set in the middle of the stage. Off to one side of the stage is an easy-chair and a telephone stand with a telephone. The time is the present, set in middle class America, Anytown, USA.

Characters:

JOHN: The father. Forty-ish. Slightly gray and wears a tank top tee-shirt the entire play. By scene 3, his hair is almost entirely gray.

MARY: The mother. Forty-ish. Wears a kitchen apron the entire play. By scene 3, her hair is gray.

CISTINE: Mary's sister. About 35 years old.

RUPERT: John and Mary's son. In scene 1 he's about 17 years old. In scene 2 he's 21. By scene 3 he's slightly gray at 40 years old and wears a tank top tee-shirt.

MISSY: Rupert's wife. In scene 2 she's 21. In scene 3 she's 40 and wears a kitchen apron.

EUGENE: Rupert and Missy's eldest child. In scene 3 he's 17 years old.

Scene 1

(John is seated at the dining room table reading the evening newspaper. Mary is setting the table for dinner.)

MARY: (looking out window) It's going to be a beautiful day tomorrow.
JOHN: (reading newspaper at table) It's supposed to rain.
MARY: It's probably best. The farmers need all the rain they can get.
JOHN: If they get any more it'll ruin the crops and prices'll skyrocket. Probably won't be able to find corn or eggplant for less than $3.80 a pound.
MARY: That's okay...I don't like eggplant anyway.
JOHN: It's good if it's fried.
MARY: You're not supposed to have fried foods.
JOHN: I'm not supposed to have a lot of things.
MARY: But you eat them anyway.
JOHN: You serve them to me!
MARY: You won't eat anything else!
JOHN: You can't *make* anything else!
MARY: Well...I hope it doesn't rain.
JOHN: It's supposed to.

(doorbell rings)

JOHN: Who the hell is that?
MARY: Probably my sister, Cistine.
JOHN: Cistine? Again? Let me guess. Your father finally came to his senses and kicked that flaming virgin out. Now she's taking up

	permanent residence with us.
MARY:	She hasn't been over *that* often.
JOHN:	You're right. Four times this week alone isn't a lot. (Mary leaves room to answer door) It's more than I see my own son.

(Mary and Cistine enter the room)

MARY:	John, look who's here! It's Cistine.
JOHN:	Big surprise.
CISTINE:	I don't think he likes me, Mary.
MARY:	Don't be silly. Of course he likes you. How could he not, you're my sister.
CISTINE:	He always ignores me.
MARY:	Not always. You remember last Monday he told you to get him a beer.
CISTINE:	Oh yes...I forgot.
MARY:	Besides, he has a lot on his mind.
CISTINE:	You mean Rupert?
MARY:	We've both been very worried.
CISTINE:	How *is* the boy?
MARY:	Getting worse, I'm afraid.
CISTINE:	It was such a shock. He seemed fine just a few days ago.
MARY:	I know. It caught us by surprise too.
CISTINE:	He's so young.
MARY:	Too young. One minute he's out running around without a care in the world, and the next minute...whamo!
CISTINE:	I'll bet it's hard on you.
MARY:	Irregular eating habits, moodiness, strange behavior...he's gone through it all.
CISTINE:	Whamo.

MARY: Whamo.
CISTINE: What are you going to do?
MARY: Do? What is there to do? Let it run its course, I suppose.
CISTINE: I hope he comes out of it. So many don't.
MARY: It's so sad. (pause) The big L.
CISTINE: The big L. I had it once. Remember? When I was about 16.
MARY: What happened?
CISTINE: Don't you remember? I couldn't eat, I couldn't sleep, it was terrible.
MARY: Yes...now I remember. Mother cried for hours.
CISTINE: I grew out of it, though.
MARY: I hope Rupert does too. He's so young.
CISTINE: Too young.
MARY: The big L.
CISTINE: Whamo.
JOHN: (setting paper down) I wish you two would stop talking about the boy as if he's got leprosy.
MARY: You can't ignore it any longer, John.
CISTINE: The big L is nothing to laugh about, John.
JOHN: Rupert is in love. That's all. L-O-V-E. Leave him alone.

(Rupert enters room)

MARY: Rupert! You don't look well.
CISTINE: Rupert, how are you?
JOHN: Don't worry son, you don't have to answer her if you don't want to.
MARY: Do you want something to eat, Rupert?

	Maybe you'll feel better. (feels Rupert's forehead)
RUPERT:	I feel fine.
CISTINE:	Of course you do, dear.
MARY:	We're having chicken with dumplings tonight!
CISTINE:	I love chicken with dumplings.
RUPERT:	I'm not hungry.
MARY:	(cries) I'll fix you something. (leaves room toward kitchen)
CISTINE:	I *love* chicken with dumplings.
JOHN:	Cistine?
CISTINE:	(excited) Yes, John?!
JOHN:	Go get me a beer, will you?

(Cistine leaves room toward kitchen)

JOHN:	Son, come here a minute.
RUPERT:	Yes, Dad?
JOHN:	Son...you can tell me. Do you have it bad, or what?
RUPERT:	Do you mean Missy? Isn't she wonderful? Her hair is like spun gold. Her teeth are like shiny pearls. Her eyes open a doorway to her very soul, and her smile...
JOHN:	Lights up a room?
RUPERT:	You noticed it too?!
JOHN:	(nods) You've got it bad.
RUPERT:	We always hold hands when we go out for a walk. It's as if we couldn't go out *unless* we held hands. Even though there may be other girls around, I never really notice them.
JOHN:	You've got it *real* bad.

RUPERT: She makes me feel like no one else exists. Like no one else matters. Like I'm the most special person in the world and everything I say is important. Can you imagine such a thing? Did you ever feel like that, Dad?
JOHN: (looks toward kitchen) Never.
RUPERT: This is great. I keep asking myself, how long can it last?
JOHN: Only until you're married, I'd say.
RUPERT: Dad, I've been giving this a lot of thought...and I think I'm going to ask Missy to marry me.
JOHN: Oh, boy. Sit down, son, I want to talk to you.
RUPERT: Don't try and talk me out of it, Dad. My mind is made up.
JOHN: Talk you out of it? I wouldn't think of it — everybody's entitled to their own mistakes. (Rupert sits) Son, before you go and do this thing there are a few things I think you should be aware of. First of all, marriage is one of those things where...ah...rather, before you consider marriage you should first ask yourself... It's much better to think of marriage as a...umm. It's not so much what marriage *is*, but what it isn't. Do you follow me so far?
RUPERT: I'm not sure.
JOHN: Good. Rupert, it's just that, as hard as we try, sometimes it doesn't seem as if it will *ever*...but then it always does. When *I* got married, I...I mean your mother...that is, we...aw forget it. Good luck, Rupert. If you

	need anything, let me know.
RUPERT:	Thanks Dad! (runs out of the room toward the front door)
JOHN:	(yells) Let that be a lesson to you!

(Mary and Cistine enter from the kitchen)

MARY:	What's all the yelling about?
JOHN:	The boy and I were having a talk.
MARY:	You should learn how to control yourself, John. You'll give yourself a heart attack. Besides, the poor dear probably didn't deserve it.
JOHN:	How do *you* know?
MARY:	He's at that age. We've got to try and be patient with him. And understanding... (John rises and places his chair directly behind her) ...and not treat him like some sort of a baby.
JOHN:	He's getting married.
MARY:	(throws up her arms and collapses into chair) My baby!

(Cistine looks on and gasps)

— BLACKOUT —

Scene 2

(It's 5 years later. Wedding march music plays in the background. A baby is born to Rupert and Missy. There is a slap and a baby cries. The room is empty. John sneaks in from the kitchen, looks around, and sits at the table with his newspaper.)

JOHN: Alone at last. There hasn't been any peace and quiet in this house since before they moved in with us. It's like living with the Brady Bunch.
MARY: (from the kitchen) John...! Can you help me?
JOHN: No, dear. I'm afraid you're beyond help.

(There's a loud crash in the kitchen. John slams paper down and leaves room for kitchen. Rupert enters room from the front door, looks around, sits at the table and starts reading the paper that John left.)

RUPERT: (sighs) Alone at last.
JOHN: (enters from kitchen) *What* are you doing?!
RUPERT: (startled — throws paper up) What?!
JOHN: What do you think you're doing? That's *my* paper and I haven't read it yet!
RUPERT: I'm sorry, Dad. I was just looking for some peace and quiet.
JOHN: In *this* house?
RUPERT: It's just that I have no time for myself anymore. I work all day, come home exhausted and she wants me to do everything around here, too. I have to go out and work on the car just to get a little privacy. 'Are you working on that *again*?' she says. I just wish I knew something about auto repair! If I try to have a beer with the fellas, she says, 'Are you going drinking *again*?' And what can I say? 'I'm going out for a good time but

	you stay here and take care of the kid.' I can't say anything, go anywhere, do anything. (pause) My God, being married is like...being dead!
JOHN:	Amen.
RUPERT:	Sometimes I just want to move out and not tell anyone where I am.
JOHN:	Don't you dare! A little while ago I was changing the diapers of a kid who isn't even mine.
RUPERT:	Sorry, Dad.
JOHN:	(pause, hands Rupert a section of the paper) Here, son. I've already read this.
RUPERT:	Thanks, Dad.
MISSY:	(from kitchen) Where is he?! Rupert!
RUPERT:	I've got to go. (stands, starts toward front door)
MISSY:	(Enters wearing curlers in her hair. Points hair dryer at him.) Freeze!! (Rupert stops) Where do you think you're going?!
RUPERT:	Going? Just out to the garage. (pulls tool from back pocket) I need to tighten up the flywheel valve on the intake manifold so the catalytic converter doesn't choke. (leaves room quickly out the front door)
MISSY:	(to John) I didn't know it was bad again. Rupert! (follows Rupert out)
MARY:	(enters holding baby, moves to center of the room) Missy? Rupert? John!
JOHN:	Mary. (holds up paper)
MARY:	Are they coming back? Am I supposed to watch the baby? Why don't they ever tell me anything? Just go and leave Grandma

	holding the kid. I don't mind, really I don't, but can't they at least tell me when they're coming back? Or even if they are coming back at all! No one ever tells me anything. It's like I'm not even in the room. John...!
JOHN:	Yes, dear.
MARY:	Yes, what?
JOHN:	Yes, they're coming back. Or I'll kill them.
MARY:	What should we do with little Eugene?
JOHN:	Put him in a basket and leave him next door.
MARY:	We can't do that.
JOHN:	You're right. We'd never get the basket back.
MISSY:	(enters from the front door) Men! A million things to be done, and they always have an important reason to disappear. If it's not one thing it's something else. Don't they think we have anything better to do than pick up after them *and* a baby?
MARY:	Sometimes they're *worse* than babies.
MISSY:	One of these days we ought to join together and rise up...
JOHN:	(looks over top of paper) I'd better go see how Rupert's coming with the car. (leaves in a hurry out front door)
MARY:	(sits with baby and feeds it with bottle) We should have the best running cars in the neighborhood, but I'm lucky if I can get to the corner store without it overheating.
MISSY:	(takes baby, sits) Did you ever wonder why God chose women to be the ones to bear children?
MARY:	I asked my mother that question once. She

	said that it was punishment for that whole "Adam and the apple" business.
MISSY:	I wouldn't be surprised.
MARY:	I don't even *like* apples. (stands to hand Missy baby bottle)
MISSY:	I'll probably never eat another one. I love our baby, though. He's so cute and fun. It's just that he's so much work. If only I got more help from Rupert. He has his hands full, I know. What with his job, and always fixing the car's cadillac inverter or whatever. I just don't know how I'm going to tell him that I think I'm pregnant again.
MARY:	(drops bottle) What?! Are you sure?
MISSY:	Well...I haven't been to the doctor yet, but I'm late like before. And I'm sick in the morning like before. And I'm depressed — just like before.
MARY:	I can't believe it! I just can't believe it! How could this happen?!
MISSY:	It's an old recipe. It's been around for years.
MARY:	I know *how* it happened, but how could you *let* it happen?
MISSY:	What do you mean?
MARY:	What do I mean? What do you mean, what do I mean?! You're newlyweds, with a newborn, living here because you can't afford a place of your own, only one job between you, you're expecting another child...and you ask me what I mean? Haven't you ever heard of condoms?!
MISSY:	Rupert's going to faint when he finds out.
MARY:	Fainting is nothing. I'm not worried about

fainting. Your father-in-law is going to have a massive coronary. Or a stroke. Maybe even a cerebral hemorrhage!

(John enters through front door)

MISSY: Is Rupert almost done out there?
JOHN: Done? Oh...it's coming along. It's a real messy job.
MISSY: (to Mary) Would you watch Eugene, please? I'm going to go talk to my husband. I'll be right back — I hope.
MARY: Sure, I'd be happy to. (Missy leaves through front door)
JOHN: 'Happy to'? A few minutes ago you were complaining about how they always dump the baby with you.
MARY: We women have to stick together. Besides the kids have it rough.
JOHN: Rough?! You call *this* rough?
MARY: I wouldn't call it high living.
JOHN: When *we* were married we didn't have the luxury of staying with our parents. Yours were divorced and mine...
MARY: Didn't want to have anything to do with us.
JOHN: ...couldn't afford to put us up. I worked two jobs to support our standard of living.
MARY: We ate baloney a lot.
JOHN: You took care of the home and the baby and never once had to leave him with anyone.
MARY: Never went anywhere, either.
JOHN: You were out almost every day.
MARY: Grocery shopping and mowing the lawn

	don't count.
JOHN:	The point is, we pulled ourselves up by our bootstraps so we wouldn't be slaves to the house or the kids. (looks at baby and scowls) *Our* kids. They can do the same thing with fortitude, determination, and hard work. Then, and only then, will they see the fruits of their labor multiply.
MARY:	Oh, they're multiplying all right. (places chair behind John)
JOHN:	What do you mean?
MARY:	She's pregnant! (John gasps, clutches chest, collapses into chair)

— BLACKOUT —

Scene 3

(It is now 17 years later. Rupert and Missy had 2 more children, Sissy and Philbert, both of whom are now teenagers and wild. John, Mary, Rupert, Missy, and Eugene are seated around the table at dinner time.)

JOHN:	Dear Lord...I thank you for this food which we are about to receive, and I ask that you bless my happy family. I'll let Rupert plead his own case.
RUPERT:	Ditto, Lord. And please bless our wonderful children...wherever they are.
ALL:	Amen.

(everyone starts reaching, grabbing, passing, etc.)

MARY:	Come to think of it, where *are* the little darlings?
JOHN:	Who's that, dear?
MARY:	Our two other grandchildren. Don't you even notice that they're not here?
JOHN:	Now that you mention it, it does seem too peaceful.
RUPERT:	Yeah. Where are they?
MISSY:	They're not here.
RUPERT:	I already know where they're *not*. What I don't know is where they *are*. Where is Sissy tonight?
MISSY:	Out.
RUPERT:	Out where?
MISSY:	Just out.
RUPERT:	Who is she 'just out' with?
MISSY:	Does she have to be going out with anyone?
RUPERT:	Who?!
MISSY:	No one you know.
RUPERT:	Why don't I know him?
MISSY:	Because she didn't think you'd like him.
RUPERT:	That is precisely the reason I want to meet him! And where is Philbert?
MISSY:	He just left.
RUPERT:	Where did he go?
MISSY:	Out.
RUPERT:	Out where?
MISSY:	Don't start.
RUPERT:	(goes to window, opens it, and shouts at Philbert who is leaving the yard) Philbert! Come back here and eat with your family for a change. Who knows, you might come to enjoy it. When are you going to spend some

time around here, young man? The lawn needs to be done, can't you see that? And the cars need to be washed. You kids don't know how good you have it! You have a roof over your head, food on your back, clothes on the table...and still you don't do anything to lift a finger around here. You're spoiled, do you hear me? Just once I'd like to see you take pride in your house. (pause) What? (pauses, then quickly turns away from the window and sits back down) Little shit.

JOHN: What did he say?
RUPERT: He said it wasn't *his* house. It was *yours*. I was going somewhere with that. I really was.
JOHN: It was a nice try though.
RUPERT: (to Eugene) You going out, too, son?
EUGENE: Me? Naw. (goes to phone, sits, makes call)
JOHN: There goes the phone.
RUPERT: There could be a national emergency, and if someone tried to call and warn us — we'd be doomed. We're isolated. No calls in or out. It's kind of frightening, y'know?

(Mary and Missy start clearing table, then go into kitchen)

RUPERT: (pointing to Eugene) Kind of reminds you of me, I'll bet.
JOHN: How so?
RUPERT: You know. Young, preoccupied, always underfoot.
JOHN: Underfoot? You? You've got to be kidding.

	You were never home. I rented your room out for a whole month before I realized you still lived here.
RUPERT:	They're a good bunch of kids though, aren't they?
JOHN:	What kids?
RUPERT:	*My* kids.
JOHN:	Yeah, they're a good bunch. In fact, in some neighborhoods they'd be considered a good *gang*.
RUPERT:	They're not *that* bad.
JOHN:	Not when you compare them to Attila the Hun, Idi Amin, or Adolf Hitler.
RUPERT:	I'd like to see Eugene get out more.
JOHN:	So would I. He's the only one worth a damn.
RUPERT:	I hate to see him wasting day after day on the telephone.
JOHN:	Especially since he doesn't have much time left.
RUPERT:	What do you mean?
JOHN:	The signs, boy — you've got to look for the signs. What do you think he's doing right now? Getting a tee-time? Discussing analytical geometry with his classmates? Finding out the relative humidity? No way. The boy's on the prowl. And that may not be all.
RUPERT:	Girls?
JOHN:	You *are* quick.
RUPERT:	Eugene? Naw, he's too young. He's only seventeen.
JOHN:	The boy is smitten. The big L. Take my word for it, I know. I've seen it. Look at

	that. (points to Eugene, now sitting upside down on chair, still talking on phone)
RUPERT:	Wow, I never noticed that before. Don't the blood rush to his head?
JOHN:	Sure it does. But if they sit up straight for that length of time all the blood drains out of their brain and they run out of things to say.
RUPERT:	I never thought about that.
JOHN:	Y'know, it's times like right now that I wish Cistine hadn't joined that convent.
RUPERT:	Aunt Cistine? You're kidding. You *hated* Aunt Cistine.
JOHN:	Yeah, but now I have to get my own beer. (leaves room toward kitchen)

(Missy enters from the kitchen and sits at the table while Rupert reads the paper)

MISSY:	Rupert? Rupert, dear, can we talk?
RUPERT:	(drops paper) Oh my God, you're pregnant!
MISSY:	No, no it's nothing like that.
RUPERT:	You about scared me half to death.
MISSY:	Rupert, I've been thinking.
RUPERT:	Uh-oh...I don't like the sound of that.
MISSY:	We never have any time for each other anymore.
RUPERT:	I knew it.
MISSY:	When was the last time we went anywhere together? Alone.
RUPERT:	Before we were married.
MISSY:	That's right. And that was only to the drive-in.
RUPERT:	So what are you saying? You want to go to

	the drive-in?
MISSY:	There are no more drive-ins, Rupert. I want us to go somewhere to be alone. Maybe we can go to a movie, sit in the back row and neck.
RUPERT:	Neck? What the heck for? We're *married*.
MISSY:	You have no romance left in you.
RUPERT:	No romance? Where do you think our kids came from?
MISSY:	Sometimes I wonder. (pause) I don't know why I try anymore. What's the use? (begins to cry) You don't care, why should *I*? I don't even know why we're together.
RUPERT:	C'mon now, don't do that. C'mon. I care. I do. It may not look like it all the time, but I care a lot. We're together because we love each other. Remember? You know...the big L. C'mon, don't cry. I hate when you do that. I love you, really. If you want to go somewhere, we'll go somewhere.
MISSY:	Alone?
RUPERT:	Just you and me, babe.
MISSY:	Do you mean it?
RUPERT:	You bet. Just like the old days.
MISSY:	Where will we go?
RUPERT:	Anywhere you want. You name it.
MISSY:	Oh, honey.
RUPERT:	Baby.
MISSY:	Sweetie.
RUPERT:	Dumplin'.
MISSY:	I love you.
RUPERT:	I love *you*.

(they stand and hug)

MISSY: I'm going to go tell Mom that we're going out on a date!
RUPERT: Okay!

(Missy heads toward kitchen)

RUPERT: Whew! (sits back down and reads paper)

(John enters room from kitchen)

JOHN: Here...this is from me. (hands him a beer). And this is from your mother. (hands him a condom)
RUPERT: Thanks.
JOHN: How's he doing? (points to Eugene, still on the phone)
RUPERT: Still breathing, I think. (reading paper) Y'know Dad, this is nice.
JOHN: (reading paper) What's that?
RUPERT: The peace and quiet. It's so relaxing.
JOHN: Yes, but how long can it last?

(Eugene hangs up phone receiver, John and Rupert immediately look over at him. Rupert checks his wristwatch.)

RUPERT: That wasn't long at all, Eugene. Is everything all right?
EUGENE: Gee Dad...I don't know.
JOHN: I don't like this.
RUPERT: Don't you feel well, son?
EUGENE: I've got a weird feeling in my stomach.

JOHN: Suddenly, I don't feel well myself.
RUPERT: You were on the phone with your girlfriend Louise, weren't you?
EUGENE: Yes...I was.
JOHN: Uh-oh, I can see this coming.
RUPERT: Son, you're not about to say that you and Louise are...getting married, are you?
JOHN: (to Rupert) Brace yourself.
EUGENE: Of course not.
JOHN & RUPERT: Whew! (toast cans of beer to each other, taking big swallows)
EUGENE: Louise is pregnant.

(John and Rupert both spray beer out of their mouths)

RUPERT: What! Are you crazy?! What's wrong with you?!
EUGENE: Nothing, apparently.
JOHN: Are you sure it's not just one of those woman's things?
RUPERT: Yeah, maybe it's just gas.
EUGENE: She saw a doctor. She's pregnant all right.
RUPERT: Shhh...! You want your mother to hear you?!
JOHN: Or worse, your grandmother?!
RUPERT: How can this happen? You're on the phone with the girl morning, noon, and night.
EUGENE: Not *every* night.
JOHN: Are you sure...you know...that you're the one?
RUPERT: Dad, will you stay out of this please? (to Eugene) Well? Are you?
EUGENE: Yes, I'm sure.
JOHN: Well, that's it then. We'll change our name

RUPERT:	and move.
RUPERT:	Don't be ridiculous, Dad. Changing our name is out of the question.
EUGENE:	Dad, what am I going to do?
JOHN:	How about suicide?
RUPERT:	(to John) Stop it. (to Eugene) What do *you* want to do?
EUGENE:	Suicide sounds good right about now.
RUPERT:	You *may* not have to worry about that! (shakes fist at him angrily)
EUGENE:	Suddenly marriage doesn't sound too bad. I wanted to marry Louise eventually anyway, this'll just push things up a little. By a few years.
RUPERT:	I think you'd be doing the right thing.
EUGENE:	What's it like...you know, being married and having kids and stuff?
RUPERT:	Son...marriage is like nothing you've ever experienced.
JOHN:	Or are ever likely to again.
EUGENE:	No, really. Is it fun?
JOHN:	(to Rupert) Do you want to handle that one, or shall I?
RUPERT:	Let me take a crack at it. 'Fun' isn't exactly the word I'd use. 'Different' is a better word. Or 'permanent,' that's a good word. So is 'surrender.'
JOHN:	'Exhausting.'
RUPERT:	'Trying.'
JOHN:	'Fragile.'
RUPERT:	'Compromising.'
JOHN:	'Exhausting.'
RUPERT:	You said that one. 'Demanding.'
JOHN:	'Constant.'
RUPERT:	'Tiring.'

JOHN:	'*Real* tiring.'
RUPERT:	Anyway...it isn't so much of what marriage *is*, but rather what it *isn't*. When I got married, or at least *before* I got married, I used to think, or at least I thought...that is, when I met your mother there were things that, well...but after we were married for a while those things didn't matter. No, there were too many other things. And so it'll probably be the same with you. Marriage, if you really think about it...ah...when people get married they don't always, I mean, *sometimes* they do, but not always. Do you follow me so far, son?
EUGENE:	I'm not sure.
RUPERT:	Hmm... (to John) I don't know.
JOHN:	You're doing fine. Keep going.
RUPERT:	Even when your grandfather got married, my mother, his wife, your grandmother...and ah...basically it was the same for me. I don't know what else I can say about it without confusing you. Good luck, son, I'll be right here if you ever need me. If you ever need to talk...or a place to stay... (John shoots Rupert a dirty look) ...ah, we'll talk about it. (Rupert shakes Eugene's hand)
EUGENE:	Thanks, Dad. Thanks, Grandpa. (leaves room toward front door)
RUPERT:	These are the happiest days of his life.

(John & Rupert look at each other, then to the front door)

JOHN & RUPERT:	(yelling) Let that be a lesson to you!!

— BLACKOUT, CURTAIN —

# # #

135

Merry New Christmas

Our story begins many years ago, in early December during the late twentieth century, at St. Christopher's seminary in the small town of Parkway, Indiana. Brother John was the newest member of St. Christopher's and considered by some to be the most eccentric. It was true that his interests ranged from astronomy to ancient history, but he felt that his devotion to his calling was just as intense.

John's assigned mentor, Father Harold, an ordained veteran of St. Christopher's, was very supportive. He defended John a number of times during those first months saying that what a person brought in from the outside often shaped the spirit within. As soon as John completed his...transformation, Harold argued, he might very well be the most devoted priest to ever graduate from St. Christopher's. Father Harold wasn't sure if anyone believed it, he wasn't sure if he believed it himself. But as a mentor, Harold was obligated to do everything in his power to see that John had a fighting chance.

The longer John was there, however, the harder it was for Harold to understand John's...diversions. After breakfast, chores, morning devotions, mass, lunch, and then afternoon devotions, John was always in the seminary library doing research; or at least that was what it appeared he was doing. He would spread at least a dozen books, articles, notepads, and folders on the table in front of him. Some seminary Brothers even said they saw him using a protractor and compass. At first, Harold thought nothing of it. An inquisitive young man, he figured.

It was only after John failed to show up for a three o'clock committee meeting for which he had volunteered, that Harold began to realize the depth of the problem.

John was sitting at his usual table in the back of the library when Harold found him. He was deep in thought, as always, and didn't notice anyone standing near him. His books and papers covered the table. Several blueprints were unrolled under his notepad. There was even a twelve inch globe on the table.

"And what might that be you're working on?"

Startled, John sat upright. "Father Harold! I didn't know you were there!"

"I'm sorry if I'm disturbing you."

"Not at all, Father. Won't you join me?"

Harold walked around the table and sat down in the chair across from the young Brother.

John set his pencil down and removed his eyeglasses. He rubbed his eyes and then suddenly looked at his wristwatch. It was 3:30.

"The meeting! I'm sorry, Father. I must have forgotten. I don't know where the time went. I'm really sorry! It won't happen again!"

He immediately stood and frantically gathered the books and papers. "If I could just have a moment, I'll be ready...if it's not too late."

"It's never too late for a new direction," Harold told him as he watched book upon book being gathered and stacked. He was fascinated by the level of interest his spiritual student had in this 'project.'

"Stop a moment, and calm down. You're making me dizzy just watching you! The committee has already adjourned. I can brief you in my office later this evening."

John sat back down disheartened. "I'm sorry, Father.

It's just that I want so much to do well here at St. Christopher's."

"Of course you do, John. And that is exactly what I want to talk to you about."

Harold picked up a few of the books that were stacked. The titles surprised him: *Astrophotography - A Global Investigation*; *World History and Pre-Modernization*; *Ancient Astrology*; *Celestial Navigation*; and *Migratory Evolution - A History*.

"Pretty heavy reading. For pleasure?"

"Ah, not exactly, Father."

"You know, John, we at St. Christopher's feel we have a very important duty. It's very simple — we train young men to be good priests. And I, as your mentor, have the responsibility of helping you achieve that end. It seems, though, I may have failed you in some way."

"What do you mean, Father?"

Harold waved his hands over the table. "All of this! It appears as if you may be...distracted from your calling. While the other boys are studying scripture, you sit in the library studying...astrology!"

"Not 'astrology,' Father, astronomy. One is the influence of stars and planets on human events, and the other is the science of the celestial bodies and of their magnitudes, motions, and constitution."

Harold felt his face tighten.

"Regardless, my son, rather than having your mind on heaven, you've got your head in the clouds! Whenever a student comes to St. Christopher's, we always expect a certain amount of personal adjustment. That's natural. You give up the only life you have ever known, filled with self-gratification, for a totally new life filled with self-sacrifice. Some young men think they are ready for the commitment ahead but find that they cannot change that easily. Some cannot change at all. For them, the calling was not strong enough. They just cannot leave the past in the past. Sooner or later they return to the familiarity of the outside, back to what they did before coming here. That does not make them bad people, or bad Christians, it just means they were not ready. You've been here nearly four months already and I'll be honest with you John, some people here at St. Christopher's don't think *you* are ready."

John leaned back in his chair. He knew he had become absorbed with his project. He even knew that it had drawn attention from the other Brothers, but he hadn't expected a reprimand from his mentor. Not yet, anyway.

"Father, I realize this all may seem a little strange. But let me assure you, I *have* dedicated my life to God. I can't begin to tell you how important being a priest is to me. While other kids were studying sports trivia, I was studying the Bible. While they practiced scrimmages and rehearsed game plays, I was playacting scenes from every movie I could think of that had a priest in it! And believe me, I've seen a lot of priest movies. Those kids wanted to be doctors, lawyers...I wanted to be a priest. No, Father, St. Christopher's is where I belong!"

Harold smiled. He had to admit, his speeches did seem to reach the wayward young men. He'd perfected it over the years, using it on dozens of boys who were...distracted. Sometimes the boys would be packed up and on their way home by that evening, and sometimes they would react as John did, with renewed enthusiasm. It made him proud.

"So now you'll gather up all your hobby material and get down to the business of God, I trust."

For the first time, John looked away. He was silent and deep in thought.

"There really is no other way, my son. We cannot serve two masters, and if your hobbies preoccupy your mind, then..."

"Father, the work I am doing is not merely a 'hobby,'" he said finally. "It is very necessary and important. I can't just pack up years of research and abandon something that is so close to changing...everything!"

Harold was sad. "I don't know what else to say, John." He stood up. "I'll have the dismissal papers prepared."

John stood up quickly. "No, Father, wait! Please. You can't expel me. At least let me explain."

Harold slowly sat down to give the boy the benefit of an explanation. Also, he didn't want to believe that his world-class speech had failed.

John looked around to see if anyone was close enough to overhear. They were alone. He sat down.

"You've got me wrong, Father. What I'm doing here is *because* of my commitment to God. And believe me it's in the best interest of St. Christopher's to let me continue."

Now Harold was confused. Just when he thought he'd figured out this boy, there was a new angle. He had to know more.

"Go on."

"For the past five years I've been working on this idea. Sort of a riddle, actually. And I think I'm very close to the answer. I was going to present it to you after I came to a conclusion, really I was, but I'm still working on it."

Harold just stared at him. If this was some sort of a stall tactic, it was one of the most unique he'd ever seen.

"Perhaps you'd better tell me what's on your mind."

John was nervous and almost apologetic. "I just didn't want to present an incomplete picture, or draw an erroneous conclusion. That's all. That's why I had to be sure."

Harold nodded, even though he had no idea why. "Of course. But if you don't tell me now, you may not be at St. Christopher's long enough to tell me later."

John lowered his voice. "When I was an altar boy, I decided to become a priest. From then on I was always the one who said grace at our meals. Well, one year, at my family's Christmas celebration, after I had just finished saying the blessing, my nine year old nephew asked me on what day Jesus was born. Naturally, I reminded him that we celebrate the birth of Jesus on December twenty-fifth. But that wasn't what he wanted to know. He wanted the day of the week. We all laughed, gave him a pat on the head, and moved on to dessert. But I couldn't get it out of my head. The next day, the next week, even a month later I was still thinking about his question. I'm not one to get caught up in trivia, but I just had to look into it."

He smiled. Harold just listened.

"I went to our church and asked our priest. He told me that there was no way to tell *exactly* which day Jesus was born, or even the date for that matter. He said that December twenty-fifth was chosen to represent that special day, and that's how it's been ever since. But with all the calendar changes before and after Caesar Augustus, and the Bible being nonspecific in this area, there was just no way to tell for sure."

Harold just kept staring. John couldn't tell if he was fascinated or bored.

"Have *you* ever wondered about this, Father?"

"Yes, I have. Yes, of course, but I also realized that there was only so much that we mortals know or will ever know. The rest, I'm afraid, is all left up to faith."

John nodded. "That's what I thought, too. But still I couldn't get this thing out of my head. I did some research and found out that some European countries used to celebrate the birth of Jesus on January sixth. But they changed the date to fall during the time that the Romans celebrated the winter solstice, pulling December twenty-fifth out of thin air, apparently.

"But what day was it *really*? I mean, why couldn't it be figured out? We know approximately the year he was born, give or take a few years, we know the rulers at the time, and we know the wise men followed a bright 'star' to his birthplace. I know that's vague, but those few puzzle pieces told me that someone *should* be able to figure it out.

"I've been to all the libraries in the county, studying ancient civilizations, astronomy, constellation migration..."

Harold finally looked away, deep in thought. When he looked back at John, the boy was grinning, certain that he'd convinced the priest of his good intentions.

"When I first saw you doing all this...research, I was certain that you were too distracted with a hobby to devote yourself to St. Christopher's spiritual doctrine. Now I know that you have, in fact, dedicated yourself to God."

John beamed. "Yes! Yes, I have!"

"I also understand now that your enthusiasm needs to be redirected."

"Father?"

"Your heart is in the right place, but for all the wrong

reasons. It is not so important *when* Jesus was born, as what he said and did while he was here. That is what you should spend your time and energy on. Redirect your study habits to the scripture and I'm convinced St. Christopher's will provide everything you want and need for your spiritual development."

Harold was quite proud of himself — another speech saved!

"But Father, you don't understand..."

"I understand quite well, John. And as far as I'm concerned, we have resolved this problem. I don't even think we have to discuss this any more."

Harold stood, reached over the table and put his hand on the boy's shoulder. "Oh, just one more thing...let's keep this to ourselves, shall we? Some of the other priests may not be as...understanding as I am. We'll just consider this a matter between you and I."

"Yes, Father."

Harold smiled, winked, and left.

As John sat there deflated, he wondered if maybe Father Harold wasn't right. Maybe he *had* been preoccupied and distracted. Certainly he was obsessed. But if the obsession kept him from his ultimate goal of preaching God's word, then how important was it? Did it really make any difference *which* day or date Jesus came to the world? It wasn't as if he couldn't pursue his research *after* he was ordained. The key point at St. Christopher's was to *get* ordained. Yes, it certainly seemed that Father Harold was right on this one.

This realization helped John focus more clearly on the immediate future, but it left him with a deep sense of loss. Postponement, he reminded himself. The world had waited this long for the answer to this mystery, it could certainly wait a little longer.

As John gathered the rest of the books and blueprints, he heard footsteps approaching from behind. Turning, he saw that it was a friend who worked in the Monsignor's office. He was carrying a package under his arm.

"I thought I would find you here!"

"Hello, Peter."

"This just came for you," he said, handing the package to John. "I'll get reassigned if the Monsignor finds out that I distributed mail before mail-call, but you said you were waiting for something special."

John stared at the box as if he'd never seen one before. Then, he set it aside. "I was, but not anymore. Thanks anyway."

He moved the package so that it was now in front of him and noted the return address: Moore Science Ltd., Boston, MA. There was no question in his mind what the package contained.

"Oh, what the heck."

John quickly opened the package, removed the packing material, and lifted out the instrument that had been carefully packed inside. He held it up and examined it closely with a genuine sense of awe.

"What's that?" Peter asked.

"A sextant. A pretty good one, actually."

"What's it for?"

"It measures angular distances. Navigators use it to observe altitudes of celestial bodies."

Peter shook his head. "Gee, John, how'd you ever get by without one?!"

But John never heard him. He was busy flipping through the instruction manual that came with it.

"Well, have fun," Peter said. "I'll see you at dinner.

And if I were you, I wouldn't be late again. Whatever you do, don't say anything about the package."

"Don't worry about *that*," John said with a hint of excitement in his voice, "and thanks."

Peter waved as he headed out, certain that his friend would never make it to ordination.

John looked at his watch. It was an hour until dinner and two hours until dark. There was still time to do a little more research!

Since having the talk with Father Harold, John had to be extra careful about when and where he did his research, but after he had gotten the sextant there was no way that he could abandon or postpone it, in spite of the consequences.

The instrument allowed him to verify the trajectory of stars and comets that were noted in the ancient writings. Once he did that, he would be able to estimate which 'star' was the one that the Wisemen most likely followed to Bethlehem.

One theory was that certain planets lined up and gave the appearance of a single bright star. Although there was evidence that the planets Jupiter and Venus did line up around 3 B.C., they would have appeared aligned only for a short time and would not have been a good directional tool for these early astronomers.

The other theory, which John supported, was that a large comet hurtling through space led them to Bethlehem. First, John had to determine which comet could have been orbiting the Earth around that period. Then, based on when that comet was sighted throughout history, and the speed at which it had to be traveling to be seen in those locations, he could trace it's path backward through space to the time of Jesus. Back to the exact day He was born, as a matter of fact.

Two weeks after he received the sextant, John made the discovery he'd prayed for. There *was* a bright comet that could be traced backward to the time of Christ, and by all calculations, would put it on a path directly above — or at least within view of — the town of Bethlehem.

The same comet was recorded as having been seen in the late eighteenth century and again in the mid-nineteenth century. Using his sextant, protractor, and calculator, he determined the speed at which the comet came full circle through the solar system. From there, it was a relatively simple job to figure out the year it appeared above Bethlehem.

He calculated the number of days that passed since the comet flew overhead, subtracted backward, and after taking leap years into account, he incorporated his findings in the calendar system used during the time of Christ. This allowed him to determine the precise day that Jesus was born.

At last he was ready to present his findings to Father Harold! Oh, how proud and excited the Father would be, John thought. This would be an historical day of monumental proportions for St. Christopher's — and the world!

"Are you insane?!" Father Harold shouted that evening when John told him the news in his office. "There's no way you could accurately determine something like that!"

"I'm sorry, Father, but you're wrong. I've triple checked all my findings, I've considered other scenarios..."

"John, my boy, I thought we talked about this. I thought we decided that it was in your best interest to concentrate on your studies."

"Yes, we did..."

"I thought this matter was over! And now you come to me and expect me to believe that you have, 'accurately' no less, determined the date of birth of Jesus. I can't believe it. Did nothing I say sink into you? I'm sorry, but I've got to seriously question your staying on here at St. Christopher's."

"Father, I know you're upset, and you probably have a right to be. In fact, I wouldn't be all that surprised if you expel me over this. But before you do, you should hear me out and take a look at my findings."

Harold shook his head. "To what end? What good would it do? It's not possible. Theologians haven't figured it out. The Dead Sea Scrolls haven't revealed it. Even the Pope himself, God bless him, has no privileged insight. How can *you*, a student of the ministry, find out what no scholars could before you?"

John thought for a moment. "Because they weren't looking in the right place?"

Harold dabbed his forehead with his handkerchief and sat down behind his desk. There was a long pause before he said anything.

"I'm probably as crazy as you are," he said, finally, "and they're surely going to send me away too, but let's see what you've got."

John smiled. He was more than pleased. Right now, this was more exciting than having audience with the Pope. He spent the next two and one half hours describing to Father Harold how he came to his conclusion. His heart raced and it was all he could do to present the facts and findings calmly and factually. Occasionally, Harold would stroke his chin and look away, indicating to John that perhaps his explanation was getting too detailed.

After presenting all the evidence he'd accumulated, John sat down, exhilarated, and feeling as if a great weight had been lifted from his shoulders. Harold, on the other hand, was exhausted. By then, he had removed his collar, sat back, and was fanning himself with one of John's notepads. The desk was covered with unrolled blueprints, charts, notes, and research books opened to pages with key passages that had been highlighted.

"Well, if nothing else, you're to be commended for your...thoroughness," Harold said, finally. "I don't know if I believe your findings. I'm not sure I even *understand* half of them, but for the sake of conversation, let's say I do. Now what?"

It was an excellent question. After all those years of hypothesizing, researching, and verifying, John had really given no thought of what to do with the conclusion, if indeed he reached one! Now that he had, he was going to need a plan.

"I guess...we...should tell someone."

Harold leaned forward. "We?"

"You *are* going to help me, aren't you Father?"

"Help you? Help you, *what*? Embarrass yourself and St. Christopher's? Who's going to believe it?"

John was shocked. "Everyone will believe it once they see the evidence. You didn't believe it either, at first."

Harold looked down at the mountain of paperwork on his desk.

"I'm not sure I believe it *now*."

John stood up and ran his hand through his hair. He walked to the window and peered out at the night sky. He began to see his years of research and a future in the ministry going up in smoke. He turned from the window.

"But why, Father? You saw all the evidence. I answered all your arguments. The answer is right there in front of you."

Harold walked over and stood next to John.

"You know how difficult it is for the church to accept change. Well, it's even harder to accept the intervention of science in the spiritual community."

"Maybe the 'spiritual community' needs a new neighbor."

Harold didn't know what to say. In his twenty-three years of being a priest he never had to deal with such a controversial subject or student. There were no prepared speeches to draw upon. No precedents to refer to. He didn't know *what* should be done, if anything.

Suddenly, John had an idea. He glanced across the room and spotted a newspaper laying on Harold's credenza. He rushed over and picked it up.

"This is it! This is the answer of what to do next! The fastest way to get the word out to the world is through the media! Of course...why didn't I think of it before?! We'll call the newspapers, it'll be on television, the radio...!"

Harold raised both hands. "Whoa there, Nellie!"

"Father, that's the best way to tell the world. The world *needs* to know."

"Maybe," Harold admitted, grudgingly. "But there's a certain...protocol necessary here. You just can't run out and do whatever you want. What you don't seem to realize is that the church is like the military. We've got our ranks, our commanders, and as with any authoritative structure, there is an approved chain of command."

Harold sat down at his desk and wiped his brow. John sat down across from him.

"Then what do we do?"

"Well, I'm not going to be the link that disrupts the chain of command. I've been in this man's church for too long not to know how things are done. And the way things are done is through procedure."

He leaned forward with a new resolve. "Okay, here's what we're going to do..."

The next day, Father Harold and Brother John met in the Monsignor's office. It took an hour for Harold to explain John's theory and conclusion to the Monsignor. He was brief and succinct, much more so than John would have liked. John stood by, ready to offer more details or a more scientific explanation but no one asked him for one. In fact, the seventy-five year old Monsignor was stone-faced throughout the meeting.

"I see. And which day *is* it?" he asked, finally.

Harold looked at John.

"By our calendar system, it would be...August eleventh," John answered.

The Monsignor's facial expression never changed as he began to drum his fingers on the desk. "August eleventh. You're quite certain about this?"

"Oh yes, Monsignor," John answered. "Quite certain."

"And you believe this to be true, Father?"

Harold paused for a moment, then nodded. "Yes, Monsignor, I do."

It was the first time John was convinced that Father Harold believed his conclusion. Up until then, he wasn't sure if he was being patronized, or just providing evidence for his expulsion. He knew that whatever happened next, he'd face it with an ally.

The silence in that office seemed to last for hours. The Monsignor stared out the window from his chair, seemingly unaware that anyone was still in the room with him.

John looked over at Harold who seemed equally confused by the Monsignor's silence.

"This is a most unusual situation I realize Monsignor," Harold said, "but what would you suggest we do now?"

The Monsignor turned his attention from the window.

"Do? I would like to suggest that we do nothing. Who would believe it? I'm sure that if I asked, you both would agree to keep this entire subject in strictest confidence and not repeat what you've told me to *anyone*. Ever. Isn't that right?"

"Of course, Monsignor. As you wish."

John shook his head. "No...I'm sorry, Monsignor, with all due respect, that *isn't* right."

"John!" Harold snapped.

"It's all right, Father, let the boy speak."

John rose and began to pace the room.

"Monsignor, I've been working on this project for quite a while. Years, in fact. Granted, I'm no scientist, but I've done my homework. I've covered all the bases. I've tied up the loose ends. And I've managed to come up with what may be the single greatest discovery since the Dead Sea Scrolls!

"When I brought this project to the attention of Father Harold, he suggested that perhaps I was misdirected and not worthy to continue on here at St. Christopher's. He may be right. But the fact of the matter is that I have uncovered an historical truth about our savior. We can't ignore that. Christians around the world have a right to know that truth. They'll *want* to know the truth. Monsignor, August eleventh represents the truth!"

The Monsignor smiled. It was an expression that neither Harold nor John expected, or had ever seen before for that matter.

"Very good. Very well put indeed! As I said, I would *prefer* to suggest we do nothing. It is sure to be a controversial subject. I *hate* controversy. But, I strongly support truth. Especially spiritual truth. Therefore, I intend to bring this revelation up to the Bishop. With your permission."

John couldn't believe it. "Yes! Yes, of course!"

"Then that is what I will do."

The Monsignor rose and walked his guests to the door.

The next day, after giving the evening devotions, Harold returned to his office to finish some paperwork. It had been a long day and there was still much to do with only a week before Christmas. He was tired and looking forward to wrapping up the day with a cup of eggnog and a book.

From the doorway, he noticed that his leather high-back chair was turned away from him. Suddenly, the chair spun around.

"Surprise!" the male occupant said, leaning forward over the desk. He was a stocky man about fifty-five years old, holding a long gray winter coat and fedora-style hat.

Harold stopped dead in his tracks. "Mayor Carlott! What a...pleasure."

The mayor rose and greeted Harold with a hearty bear hug. "Merry Christmas, Father! I brought my annual Christmas present. Can you believe it's Christmas already?"

"Time certainly does seem to fly," Harold said, a little annoyed by Carlott's abrupt appearance.

"It's nice to see you again, Father," Carlott said, taking his place back in Harold's chair. "You're looking well. Are you exercising or just abstaining from the house desserts?"

"Neither, I'm afraid. But thank you for saying so."

"Brought you some fruit," Carlott said, setting a basket on the desk. Harold reached across the desk and snatched his reading glasses just in time or they would have been smashed by the large cellophane-wrapped basket.

"Thank you. I'll be sure to pass it around at breakfast tomorrow morning. Everyone will be very thankful."

Carlott rose and walked over to the window and pulled aside the curtain to watch ten or twelve carolers singing 'Silent Night' on the lawn. "Isn't it wonderful?" he asked. "I love this time of the year."

Harold joined the mayor at the window. "Yes, it is certainly something special. The faces change every year, but the music is always just as lovely."

"What...? Oh, right," Carlott said. "they're nice too. I was talking about Christmas. Presents! Gift-giving! Every year people brave the elements just to buy presents for their loved ones. If the economy is bad and people are out of work, they give to bring a little joy to their lives. If the economy is good, they give to spread the guilt. The merchants thrive, the local economy grows no matter what, and the taxes roll in. I love it!"

Carlott raised his arms and proclaimed through the closed window toward the carolers, "Merry Christmas, to all!"

"Mayor, your sensitivity touches us all." Harold said sarcastically, as he went and sat at his desk.

"I'm that kind of guy," Carlott said, after closing the curtains. "So what's this I hear about Christmas being cancelled next year?"

Harold sat forward, feeling a little nervous. "What...whatever do you mean, Mayor?"

"Oh, cut the malarkey, Father. I know all about our little rabble-rouser here at St. Christopher's. I got a call from the Bishop's office. Said there was some controversy brewing over at the seminary. Controversy isn't a word I like to hear, especially at this time of the year. So I stopped at the Monsignor's office on the way over to yours. He told me all about this kid's claim that December twenty-fifth isn't Christmas."

Harold slumped back in his chair. "Oh, that."

"Yes, *that*! Well, it's poppycock, I tell you. Poppycock! You certainly don't encourage this...treasonous slander, do you Father?"

"Encourage? Certainly not!"

"That's good..."

"But, the boy *has* made a fairly convincing case..."

Carlott suddenly slammed his palm down on the desk.

"I don't care if he's gotten this 'theory' from the mouth of God! I'll not tolerate anything, or anyone, interfering with the most joyous and sacred of holidays."

"Or the most profitable," Harold added, softly.

"Right! Do I make myself perfectly clear?"

Harold's face tightened. "Do I understand you to say...?"

Carlott seemed to relax, feeling the advantage had just swung his way.

"You understand me quite well, I suspect, Father. A lot of contributions come to St. Christopher's over the course of the year. From private donations, merchants, and, lest we forget, the mayor's office. If the economy were to tighten and that money were to dry up, St. Christopher's could likely find itself in a position of having to trim back. Or close it's doors entirely!"

Harold stood up. "Mayor Carlott! We at St. Christopher's certainly appreciate your many years of...support. But if you think I can be pressured to take a stance contrary to my convictions, you are sadly mistaken!"

"You're right, Father," Carlott said, putting on his hat and coat. "I'm sorry if it sounded like I was pressuring you. I realize you have no real authority here at the seminary. That's why I've already conveyed my concerns to the Monsignor. I suspect there will be a great deal to talk about tomorrow at the hearing. See you then!"

After Carlott left, Harold sat back down and sighed heavily. Looking upward he said, "Any time you want to intervene, I think we can use the help!"

The next afternoon, a long white limousine pulled up in St. Christopher's courtyard, followed by a black one just as long. Three distinguished looking business executives, including Mayor Carlott, exited the limousines while a half dozen or more seminary students looked on. The executives paraded by with their briefcases, directly into the Monsignor's office.

The Monsignor was waiting along with Father Harold, John, and Father Dykus, a representative from the Bishop's office.

"Good day," the mayor said, entering the office. He proceeded to introduce Nancy Wills, his Chief of Commerce Trade; and Earl Cavenaugh, the President of the Chamber of Commerce.

"Now, before we get started...," Carlott began.

"One minute, mayor!" the Monsignor interrupted. "Please remember this is *my* meeting, to which I've invited *you*. I will conduct it the way I see fit."

Carlott nodded and sat down in one of the two chairs facing the Monsignor's desk. Wills and Cavenaugh sat on the couch.

"First and foremost, I want to say that you have all been invited here under the clear understanding that we are to keep this discussion between ourselves until we can come to an agreement — and then do only as we are advised by the bishop's office."

Father Dykus nodded in agreement. Mayor Carlott nodded also, as did the others.

He continued. "Presuming for a moment that Brother John's calculations and hypothesis are correct..."

"I put a call in to the Adler Planetarium in Chicago," Carlott interrupted. "An astronomer there owes me a favor. I gave him the particulars of this case and after he considered the kid's theory, he gave me a big fat 'Maybe.'"

"As I was saying," the Monsignor continued, "presuming that the hypothesis is correct..."

Carlott stood up. "Presuming it's correct, we *strongly* object to anyone else finding out!"

Nancy Wills leaned forward. "Monsignor, try to understand that the Christmas shopping season, which goes from November twenty-third through December twenty-fourth, represents fifty percent of the entire annual revenue generated by the merchants of Parkway. That equates to just over thirty-five million dollars. Nine percent of that revenue goes toward financing the high cost of government in the way of taxes. Without that money the entire community will be adversely affected."

Earl Cavenaugh agreed. "Over twenty thousand people are employed by the merchants in Parkway and the surrounding communities. Their livelihoods depend on the Christmas shopping season. They squeak by the rest of year because they know that those thirty days at the end of the year make up for all the downturns. How many people will be thrown out of work if there is no sales boost in December?"

Carlott paced the floor. "Monsignor, if there is no Christmas shopping, everyone suffers. The stores, the citizens, the government, and even St. Christopher's."

John, sitting on the opposite side of the room, spoke up. "Monsignor, no one is suggesting doing away with Christmas. What we're talking about is Christian truth. And if the truth is that we should recognize the birth of the Christ child on a day other than December twenty-fifth, then don't we owe it to Him and Christians around the world to be accurate?"

The mayor turned sharply toward John. "Accurate? What's accurate, kid? Why do we celebrate half of what we celebrate on the days we celebrate them? Because of convenience. That's why. It gives people a day off of work to reflect, pray, or shop. We pick the days we want our holidays to fall on. So what if Jesus was born on a different day? No one cares."

Harold stood. "I tend to agree with John, Monsignor. I think that truth, no matter *what* the truth is, should be shared."

The Monsignor rubbed his chin. "Yes. We preach truth, and the faith in it. If we are to believe John's conclusion, then it may very well draw more borderline believers into the fold. It might even help show the nonbeliever that the church and the science communities are not that far apart."

"Changing the date of Christmas, or even indicating that we've been wrong to celebrate on the twenty-fifth, will destroy commerce in this country," Carlott protested. "If the tax base decreases, it will affect funding for schools, sewers, water treatment facilities, and road repairs. Who's going to tell the voters, I mean the taxpayers, that Christmas won't be in December anymore? That there will never be another white Christmas? That they'll have to put up Christmas decorations in shorts and tee-shirts?!"

At this point, Father Dykus spoke up. "This claim will need to be substantiated, I assure you. But from the position of the Bishop's office, even if the evidence holds up, we cannot justify or support changing the date of the Christmas observance for any reason."

"But Father...," John began.

"Let me finish. It would serve no good to the community by disrupting one of the most beloved and anxiously awaited days of the year. For generations, the date of December twenty-fifth has come to indicate more than just the birth of Jesus Christ. It is a day of peace, of reflection, and divine worship. Millions, nay, *hundreds of millions* of worshipers look forward to that one particular date. After all the calls we received when we changed our masses from Latin to English, I can just imagine what we'd hear if we even *suggested* changing the date of Christmas!"

Carlott, smug and smiling, put a cigar in his mouth. "So that's that!" He stood and began putting on his coat. His colleagues did the same.

"Is that right, Monsignor?" John asked quickly. "Is that the end?"

The Monsignor nodded. "I'm afraid so. We are guided by the directives from the Bishop's office. The Christmas celebration will remain on December twenty-fifth."

Carlott, now buttoning his coat, shook the hand of Father Dykus. "Tell the Bishop that the mayor's office appreciates the stand you have taken and that I'll show that appreciation in a more monetary form right after the holiday."

"Thank you, mayor. We *are* talking about putting an addition on our building sometime next year..."

Harold, feeling like he'd just lost a battle of his own undertaking, patted young John's shoulder. "You put up a brave fight, son, I'm proud of you. I know you'll make a fine priest someday."

"Thank you, Father Harold. There's just no fighting City Hall, is there?"

Harold shook his head. "Neither one of them, I'm afraid. We must face bureaucratic obstacles everywhere we go in life. How we deal with them either strengthens us, or drives us mad."

"At least *we* all know the truth," John said. "I think I will still recognize His birth on August eleventh, even if I have to do it through silent prayer."

Harold nodded slowly, certain they'd pursued the subject as far as the Monsignor would allow, but understanding how the young student must feel. Suddenly, he had a thought.

"Of course, that's it!" he nearly shouted.

Carlott stopped at the door, as did his associates and Father Dykus.

"Monsignor, if the major objection to revealing this information is that it would disrupt both tradition and commerce, then maybe we need to look not at changing the Christmas celebratory day, but rather adding another Christmas holiday to the year!"

Carlott removed the cigar from his mouth and slowly walked back toward the chair he had been sitting in. "Celebrate both? Preposterous! Who would tolerate two shopping days? Hey...wait a minute! Nancy, what do you think?"

Wills nodded. "That *would* double the shopping season, allow for better shopping weather, and could very well help avoid the midsummer revenue dip we experience every year."

Carlott pointed his cigar at Cavenaugh. "You?"

"On a local level it would increase store traffic," he said. "On a large scale, it could be the economic boost that the entire country needs. Think about what the country's GNP would look like after *two* Christmas holidays!"

"I don't think I like the idea of twice the amount of commercialism," John interjected.

"Take the good with the bad, kid," Carlott told him.

The Monsignor scratched his chin. "We would have twice the opportunity to talk of Jesus's ministry on Earth. Twice the opportunity to recruit new church members... there would be a rebirth of spiritualism. It has possibilities!"

Wills, now sitting, said, "We'd have to be careful not to offend the Jewish community."

"Oh, yes, that just wouldn't do," Cavenaugh said.

"We would be admitting a great deal of confidence in science," Father Dykus said. "We *could* be encouraging discussion about the whole evolution theory again. Just at a time when no one really talks about it anymore. I don't know if it's such a good idea."

John stood up. "Monsignor, many people are trying to get closer to God any way they can. Why should we deny them something spiritual that we can now offer? I say we give them August eleventh as a Holy Day of Obligation...or whatever. They'll pray, worship, feel charitable. Then on the twenty-fifth of December, they can do the whole gift-giving thing without feeling that the commercialism has ruined the spiritual part of the holiday."

Carlott tapped his chin with his cigar. "Two Christmases. One for spiritual celebration and one for gift giving. Of course, a lot of people will give presents on *both* days. I can live with that!"

"Yes, I think that would be the best alternative," the Monsignor agreed.

Wills and Cavenaugh also agreed.

"Father Dykus?" Harold asked, uncertain about the Bishop's position.

There was a long silence. "I think this may be acceptable to the Bishop," he said, finally. "In fact, I'm sure that he will present this suggestion to the Board of Regents. If they concur, they will bring the matter to his holiness, the Pontiff. We may very well see a sweeping change across the country, or even the world, in the way we celebrate the birth of Jesus. All because of you, John. You are to be congratulated. I wouldn't be surprised if you receive a call from the Bishop himself. Or perhaps even the Pope!"

John was elated. He knew that his many years of research were at last paying off. The recognition would be exciting and most appreciated, but that wasn't why he started the project in the first place. He did what he felt compelled to do and he accomplished his goal. That was reward enough.

The next few minutes in the office were joyous ones. Everyone shook hands and wished each other happy Christmas greetings. It was a touching moment.

Six months after that initial meeting in the Monsignor's office, the Board of Regents met. Fourteen Bishops and nine Cardinals met for five days discussing many subjects including the 'proposed rescheduling of Christ's birth,' or 'New Christmas' as it was being dubbed. There were many arguments over this subject, ranging from the accuracy of the conclusion to the audacity of it being claimed from a student priest.

Brother John was not allowed to attend the meeting. Neither was Father Harold nor the Monsignor. John knew that their absence virtually ensured that the concept of New Christmas would never pass. And he was right. The call came to the Monsignor who told Harold who told John. The subject was too speculative, too controversial. Even though the evidence indicated that the conclusion was based in fact, it was better in the Board's opinion to not disrupt the status quo when dealing with the universally accepted date of Jesus's birth.

The Monsignor and Harold were both disappointed, but neither was very surprised. John wasn't disappointed, because he didn't *really* expect anything to come of his discovery. He was relieved in many ways. He wasn't going to be expelled. He would, in all likelihood, be ordained by the end of the year. And he'd fulfilled his dream by unraveling a spiritual mystery. He was proud of his achievement and knew that he was ready for whatever spiritual assignments would be directed his way.

Weeks later, John received a certified copy of the letter that was sent to the Pope by the Board of Regents. In it, they discussed the possibility that Jesus was born on August eleventh — by our calendar system — and that it was a subject that should be discussed at greater length, sometime in the future. John was not mentioned by name.

The Monsignor was so impressed with John's research and diligence, that he took it upon himself to proclaim August eleventh to be 'New Christmas' at St. Christopher's. It would be a day of prayer and charity.

Mayor Carlott supported the proclamation and encouraged the local media to publicize St. Christopher's observances. They did, and it wasn't long before the residents of Parkway embraced the concept of celebrating the birth of Jesus on August eleventh. Students of St. Christopher's went out in force and performed numerous acts of volunteer work and social service over and above their normal obligations.

"It is a special day of recognition and appreciation for Jesus," the Monsignor told the reporters. "It is our belief that He may have actually been born on this day. Although it has not been confirmed by the Pontiff, we wish to honor that belief."

The townspeople didn't care if it had the Pope's blessing or even his knowledge. They took to the celebration with great enthusiasm and joined in by performing acts of kindness and charity. The local blood bank reported an increase in donations; homeless shelters had stocked shelves for the first time in years; and other charitable organizations recorded increases in contributions and volunteers. Church attendance doubled.

The first observation of August eleventh as New Christmas was so popular, that St. Christopher's and the townspeople now look forward to that special celebration each year.

No decorations are displayed on this day. No gifts are exchanged. But something magical happens to the residents of Parkway in late-summer. They reach inside to give something of *themselves*, rather than a gift from a store. The St. Christopher's seminary rings their chapel bells non-stop for twelve hours that day and for a short time the world feels like Christmas without the glitter.

So, if you are ever traveling on Interstate 38 headed for some beachside resort in early August and you happen to pull into the little town of Parkway, Indiana, don't be too surprised if almost everyone you meet greets you with a hearty, "Merry New Christmas!" Consider staying a while. They will be more than happy to tell you how their lives were changed by this wonderful spiritual event. And how it was given to them as a gift many years ago by a priest who was almost expelled from the seminary.

# # #

From the author of *Tall Tales & Short Stories*:

Rhyme & Reason
a collection of poems

by

tom catalano

A variety of light, easy to read rhyming poems on the subjects of: Christmas, love, time, nature, travel, work and much more. You'll laugh, you'll reflect, you may even feel wonderfully sentimental. But one thing you *won't* be is bored!

"96 pages, 8 chapters, 100% fun!"

■ ■ ■ ■ ■ ■ ■ ■ ■ ■ ■ ■ ■ ■ ■ ■ ■ ■ ■

Please rush me _____ copies of **Rhyme & Reason** at $11.70 each, including shipping. Illinois residents must add $0.67 sales tax. I have enclosed a check made payable to **Wordsmith Books** in the amount of $_____ .

Full Name: _____

Address: _____

City: _____ **State:** _____

Zip Code: _____

Telephone #: _____

For an order of ten or more books we offer a discount. Please write to us for details.

Wordsmith Books
P.O. Box 7394
Villa Park, Illinois 60181

From the author of *Rhyme & Reason*:

TALL TALES
&
Short Stories

by
tom catalano

Now, the author who captured your heart and made you laugh with his popular book of rhyming poetry, *Rhyme & Reason*, has you sitting on the edge of your seat with *Tall Tales & Short Stories*. Whether your favorite reading subjects are humor, science fiction, horror, suspense, or general interest...you'll find what you are looking for in this diverse collection of short fiction.

Tom Catalano has a unique style of drawing you into his imagination with story lines that are easy to read, and which will surprise and entertain you!

"176 pages, 13 stories, full of mystery and imagination!

━━━━━━━━━━━━━━━━━━━━━━━━━━━━

Please rush me _____ copies of *Tall Tales & Short Stories* by **Tom Catalano** at $12.95 each, (includes shipping and handling). Illinois residents must add $0.74 sales tax. I have enclosed a check made payable to Wordsmith Books in the amount of $_____ .

Full Name:_____

Address:_____

City:_____ **State:**_____ **Zip Code:**_____

Telephone #:_____

For an order of ten or more books we offer a discount. Please write to us for details.

Wordsmith Books
P.O. Box 7394
Villa Park, IL 60181